America's publisher of contemporary romance offers you each month six of the finest love stories:

SILHOUETTE ROMANCES.

These novels were written by the best of today's romance authors—with the American woman in mind. Silhouette Romances are sensuous and romantic without resorting to violence or strong description. They feature feminine heroines, masculine heroes and fascinating plots that take the reader across America and to the four corners of the earth.

If you believe in romance the way it used to be, read Silhouette Romances, stories of men and women in love, written especially for today's woman.

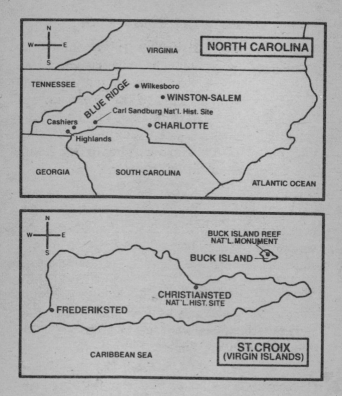

NORTH CAROLINA

VIRGINIA

TENNESSEE

BLUE RIDGE

• Wilkesboro

• WINSTON-SALEM

Carl Sandburg Nat'l. Hist. Site

Cashiers

• CHARLOTTE

Highlands

GEORGIA

SOUTH CAROLINA

ATLANTIC OCEAN

BUCK ISLAND REEF
NAT'L. MONUMENT

BUCK ISLAND

CHRISTIANSTED
NAT'L. HIST. SITE

• FREDERIKSTED

CARIBBEAN SEA

ST. CROIX
(VIRGIN ISLANDS)

"Where Have You Been?"

he demanded harshly, "as if I didn't know!"

"You don't understand . . ." Ivy began frantically as he pulled her forcefully through the door and slammed it behind her.

"Oh? *I* don't understand what it's like for you to be able to see your lover . . ."—he spat out the word—". . . whenever the mood strikes you? Did I put on the robes of celibacy along with my blindfold?"

"Please let me go, Hunter," she begged, feeling his hands on the belt of her housecoat.

His mouth came down on hers with a passion that was all but out of control.

"Was that what you went out for?" he said. "You might try the homegrown variety first—you *could* come to appreciate it."

Dear Reader:

Silhouette Romances is an exciting new publishing venture. We will be presenting the very finest writers of contemporary romantic fiction as well as outstanding new talent in this field. It is our hope that our stories, our heroes and our heroines will give you, the reader, all you want from romantic fiction.

Also, *you* play an important part in our future plans for Silhouette Romances. We welcome any suggestions or comments on our books and I invite you to write to us at the address below.

So, enjoy this book and all the wonderful romances from Silhouette. They're for *you!*

Karen Solem
Editor-in-Chief
Silhouette Books
P.O. Box 769
New York, N.Y. 10019

DIXIE BROWNING
Journey to Quiet Waters

Silhouette *Romance*

Published by Silhouette Books New York

America's Publisher of Contemporary Romance

For Lee, who taught me the meaning of the word.

Other Silhouette Romances by Dixie Browning

Chance Tomorrow
Tumbled Wall
Unreasonable Summer

 SILHOUETTE BOOKS, a Simon & Schuster Division of
GULF & WESTERN CORPORATION
1230 Avenue of the Americas, New York, N.Y. 10020

Copyright © 1981 by Dixie Browning
Map copyright © 1981 by Tony Ferrara

Distributed by Pocket Books

ISBN: 0-671-41331-7

First Silhouette Sampler Edition January, 1981

10 9 8 7 6 5 4 3 2 1

America's Publisher of Contemporary Romance

Printed in the U.S.A.

Chapter One

Poised on the stair landing, Ivy turned for one last, swift look before going up to dress. She had fairly flown through the past few days, buffing and polishing every facet of Rougemont in readiness for the party. Ruefully, she glanced down at her size-five espadrilles, scuffed and slightly frayed, and wondered how she was going to manage to keep a smile on her face as she welcomed the guests in half an hour; she ached in every bone from the work she had put in getting ready.

It was worth it. From the beveled glass panels beside the front door that sparkled against the soft, autumn tapestry beyond, to the impossibly large kitchen, where even now the caterers were stuffing ham biscuits and slicing into the wheel of cheese, Rougemont reflected the pride of generations of de Courseys.

Not that it still belonged to a de Coursey, Ivy reminded herself deliberately, biting on the pang of guilt as if it were a touchy tooth.

7

"Get a move on, Ivy," Finley called from upstairs.

She grasped the banister and forced her body up to the second floor, answering him as she went: "Ready in ten minutes, Fin. I tried the phone again and it's still out of order."

"Afraid of last minute cancellations?"

"Nope. Not afraid of anything tonight," she called through the golden oak door at the other end of the hallway. Finley had taken his clothes into the unused master bedroom this afternoon and was now changing from the old corduroys he had worn while helping her shift furniture for dancing, into the pale-blue denim leisure suit he had treated himself to for his birthday.

In her own room, Ivy took down her two-year-old dark-green gauze. It was still her favorite dress, simply cut but extremely flattering, its bias layers skimming her hips to swirl about her ankles in a way that made her feel deliciously feminine. As she brushed her heavy auburn hair and fashioned it into a coil at the back of her head, a secret smile touched her wide, full lips.

Finley. A special surprise he had said, but when she demanded to be told immediately he put her off, flashing a white, teasing smile at her.

She spread the fingers of her left hand and tried to imagine a modest solitaire sparkling there on her third finger, but it was no use. For too many years now she had waited for Fin to indicate in some way a change in their relationship, only to be disappointed as he continued to treat her exactly as he had years ago, when they ran wild through the Rougemont acres, pretending to be the first Lionel de Coursey, who had come up from Louisiana to settle on the banks of the Yadkin River, and his wife, Gillian, who had worked beside him to clear the land, borne him one son, and later scandalized the countryside by racing her mule team against that of an Iredell County tobacco farmer.

"Get a move on, gal," Fin called from outside her door. "I want you downstairs when my surprise shows up."

When his surprise showed up! That hardly sounded like an engagement ring. Some of the bright expectation fled from the evening and she sighed and peered into the mirror at the generous display of freckles adorning her small, plain face. It was the same face that had stared back at her year after year, with maturity only serving to hollow the cheeks beneath her rather elegant bones and add depth to the large, gray-green eyes in their bed of lush, dark lashes. If her nose had only been a fraction longer and her mouth a fraction smaller, she thought with resignation, she might have achieved some sort of looks. Even so, there were still those awful freckles. Sunspots, Fin had always called them.

Closing the door behind her, she wafted down the hall in a faint cloud of Odalesque. Fin had already gone down and Ivy noticed with an indulgent moue that he had left the lights on in the room he had changed in. She moved swiftly to the door and reached inside for the light switch, conscious of several things at once; of the sharp scent of masculine cologne instead of the more familiar lavender of her grandmother's time, and of the strewn clothing and toilet articles, indicative of Finley's usual haste and untidiness.

Shaking her head, she flipped the switch and moved toward the stairs. She was well aware of the fact that even now, Finley was not above a spot of fantasy concerning Rougemont. If it made him happy to imagine himself the lord and master instead of the son of her grandfather's onetime tenant farmer, then who was she to deny him that pleasure? His own old homestead was now only a chimney in the middle of a cornfield now that his parents had moved closer to town. Squaring her small shoulders, she went to greet the first guests.

Hours later Ivy flopped on the sofa and kicked off her sandals to massage her aching feet. Was there anything more dismal than the aftermath of a party? It had not even been that great a party; most of the guests were friends of Fin's; Ivy had long since lost track of her few friends in the nearby towns.

Doubts and misgivings came pouring in as, exhausted and disappointed, she relaxed amidst half-eaten food and empty, wet glasses jumbled untidily among overflowing ashtrays. She had been a fool to let Fin talk her into giving the party, just because his apartment was so small and she lived all alone here at Rougemont, and—don't deny it, Ivy, she chided herself—she could never deny Finley Hooper anything he asked of her. She had given in against her better judgment and allowed him to send out a couple from town with food and drink and to call all his friends to help celebrate his twenty-sixth birthday.

It had seemed so harmless at the time, for more than once he had brought friends and clients out to meet Ivy de Coursey of the old de Coursey homestead. She had not failed to notice that he never mentioned her position as housekeeper, but then, what harm did it do?

Oh, well, she sighed, tomorrow's another day. She stood and stretched, sandals dangling from one finger, and headed slowly for the stairs, her bare feet silent on the gleaming parquet floors. Finley had promised to try to find a cleaning woman to help her put the place together again, but she was not counting on finding one. Rougemont was too far off the beaten track for easy access and few people would bother to come all that way for a day's work.

It had been this very situation that had given Ivy the opportunity to come home again as housekeeper after Rougemont had been sold to a company called HS Engineering.

Tired to the point of distraction, Ivy's mind ranged back nostalgically over the past few years. Just out of high school, she had been called on to nurse her bedridden grandmother and within a year of Hannah de Coursey's death, Ivy's grandfather had followed. His going had been as easy and as natural as the falling of a leaf in autumn; nevertheless, it had shaken Ivy's secure little world to its foundation.

Her father, whom she had seen so few times in her life, came home bringing his thin, nervous, second wife and their two small sons. It was impossible for Ivy to comprehend their relationship and matters were not helped by the fact that Ivy was distraught and the children, feeling lost in the large old house, had clung to their mother's skirts and whined most of the time. During that tragic visit Ivy had noticed that her father could not bear to look at her. She knew she looked like her mother, who had died at her birth, and she found it somehow comforting to realize that her father had cared so deeply for the young bride he had taken when he was twenty-four.

Her father, a tall, dour man, had awkwardly offered Ivy anything she chose to take from the home as a remembrance, but Ivy had shaken her head blindly, knowing instinctively that to take one thing would be to lose it all. Better to walk away and retain it all in her heart than to try to choose.

Rougemont had been put up for sale as it stood, with Finley's firm handling the sale as soon as the estate had been settled. There were few offers for such an impractically large place in such an isolated location. It was not until over a year after the estate had been listed for sale that a representative from HS Engineering had made an offer. The money from the sale had put Ivy through secretarial school and, she assumed, insured the future for her two small half brothers up in Boston.

Ivy's rise from the typing pool at Lancing Wholesale had taken almost two years, but her position as secretary to the president, Alan Lancing, had lasted only six weeks, ending suddenly when Alan, a married man with two children in high school, had developed a rather insistent tendresse for his young secretary. After a particularly harrowing event, she had told him exactly what he could do with his job and stormed out, forfeiting a week's salary in lieu of notice. Nor had there been a possibility of any reference, since there was no higher court of appeal at Lancing Wholesale.

Finley, her port in a storm, had offered the ideal solution: "I've had three housekeepers out there since HS bought the place and I can't make 'em stick. Even old Mattie tried it, but she says it's just not the same without Lionel and Hannah."

Mattie had been the cook and housekeeper at Rougemont for as long as Ivy could remember, but those last few years had been hard on her.

"Come on, Ive, say you'll do it. HS Engineering gave us the handling of staff because we handled the sale, but if we can't cough up, we lose the account and I'm hoping it will lead to something bigger. They buy property like this all over the country, you know, strictly as an investment. Engineering's the least of their concerns now, according to the financial page."

Still Ivy had hesitated, not knowing how she could go home again as an employee, but in the end, of course, Finley had won out.

"No one to bother you, Ive, and I'll be much closer. Why, I'll be able to run out there several times a week. Nobody from HS ever even remembers that they own the place so you won't have much to do . . . that is unless the big man decides to use it as a love nest." He had laughed with something akin to envy as he proceeded to tell her about the romantic prowess of the young tycoon whose reputation for beautiful women was legend. "You can set up your jewelry equipment again in the shed and pound away to your heart's content as long as you don't burn the place down."

She had said yes, of course. After the cheap apartment in Charlotte, noisy from the nearby highway and crowded with the two other girls who pooled their rent money to be able to afford the place, all she wanted to do was to bury herself in the soft, quiet countryside at Rougemont and spend her days caring for the old house she loved with such a fierce pride. She could wander the fallow fields and riverbanks unbothered by the rushing crowds that had withered her soul.

And of course, she could see Finley, whom she had idolized for as long as she could remember.

By now, most of her dreams had eroded; tonight's "surprise" had simply swept away the dust. The only thing surprising about it had been that Finley believed she would be pleased, she thought bitterly. How could he even imagine she would welcome the news of his move to Orlando after the first of the year? The "surprise," of course, had been Sam MacNeely, an obviously prosperous realtor from Florida who had taken Finley under his pin-striped wing.

"Ivy, meet Sam MacNeely." Fin had introduced them jovially. "Sam, this is the little girl I grew up with here at Rougemont. Quite a place, isn't it? They don't make 'em the way they used to."

"Not here in the outer sticks, perched up on top of a red mud hill like a brick wedding cake, they don't!" Sam had laughed, calling his daughter over to meet their hostess.

Seated on the side of her bed as she brushed her hair, Ivy bristled at the thought of Micki MacNeely. While it might have been Sam who offered Fin the job in Orlando, it was his sugarplum fairy of a daughter who had put the idea in his head, Ivy would be willing to bet!

She had told herself she was too tired to dance, anyway, but that didn't make it any the less hurtful to watch Finley's bright blond head towering over Micki's equally bright blond head as they circled the floor in slow motion.

Sam had smiled on them indulgently as, drink in hand, he had leaned against the mantel talking politics in an overloud, overassured voice to anyone who would listen. If real estate had bought the ostentatious diamond that glittered on his little finger, then Finley was indeed chopping in high cotton, Ivy thought with uncharacteristic rancor.

Sleep fell on her like some smothering cloud and her dreams were troubled as she struggled subconsciously to gather up the threads of the past and weave them into some kind of future. Finley's Hollywood-handsome face flashed in and out of her dream with Micki's shrill laughter in the background, and around the whole she felt a somber dark cord, drawing tighter and tighter, binding her to Rougemont and her past.

She fought her way to the surface of reality with a vague sense of having been summoned. She waited, half aware, for a certain sound to repeat itself.

There it came again—a pounding and the unfamiliar ringing of the doorbell.

But no one ever came to Rougemont. No one, that is, except Fin, and he always rapped once then let himself in, for Ivy was not in the habit of locking doors unless she went into town for something.

Struggling to a sitting position, she squinted at the unusually high angle of the sun that filtered through the bare branches of the sycamore just outside her window. Who on earth could it be at this hour?

"The cleaning woman!" she exclaimed, scrambling out of bed and racing for the stairs. Fin had promised to send someone to help put the place back together again; she had forgotten all about it!

"I'm coming, I'm coming. . . . Just a minute!"

She threw open the door, apologizing breathlessly for not having heard the doorbell sooner, and found herself confronting a solid wall of pale-blue silk and dark-gray worsted, centered by a tie she instinctively recognized as being horribly expensive.

Startled, she raised her eyes, only to be jolted by a formidable jaw, a grim mouth bracketed by deeply etched lines that fell from a proud nose, and a pair of the coldest gray eyes she had ever encountered. The whole was topped off by a thatch of black hair that glinted faintly with silver.

She had never seen the man before in her life and what he was doing here on her doorstep at this hour of the morning was beyond her. He was certainly not here to wish her a good day, for he seemed to be containing his temper with the greatest difficulty. Ivy was dimly aware that temper or no temper, he was the most stunningly attractive man she had ever encountered.

Except for Finley, of course, she added hastily to herself.

"G-good morning," she croaked weakly, backing away from a situation she felt in no condition to deal with. Something in his arrogant stance and those impaling eyes started a trembling deep inside her.

"I presume you're the housekeeper's child. Does your mother sleep until noon, as well?" He stepped forward and it was either give way or risk a collision; Ivy gave way.

"I'm . . . uh . . . the housekeeper," she admitted shakily. Seldom had she felt at such a disadvantage and that feeling was not improved as she suffered his insolent eyes to drop the length of her, clad, as she was, in thin white nylon pajamas.

Those same ice-colored eyes returned to her face, taking in at one glance her display of freckles and her sleep-tousled hair, now in one fat braid over her shoulder.

"I don't think I understood you. The housekeeper?" he demanded with a withering look of disbelief. "There's been some sort of mistake. The agent . . . Hooper, I think his name was . . . was supposed to install someone responsible in here until I could get staff up from Atlanta."

As he moved toward the living room, Ivy's sleep-dazed mind snapped into awareness and she reached out to him.

"Would you like . . . uh . . . coffee, sir? In the library?"

He was obviously connected with HS Engineering, and of all the impossible times to show up, this was the worst!

He ignored her as if she had not spoken and moved to stand in the doorway, his glance taking in the dreadful remains of last night's party. In the cold light of day, it looked even worse!

After a moment that seemed to stretch to incredible lengths he turned back to where she still stood, frozen from embarrassment. "You're fired," he said dispassionately.

For a minute it didn't register. Then, when it did, Ivy began to protest: "Oh, but you can't . . ."

"I can and do."

"But I can explain. . . ." she began, only to be interrupted.

"You are no longer employed by HS Engineering, Miss . . . whatever your name is. You were obviously a last resort and I'm sorry if it inconveniences you, but Hooper had no business hiring someone so obviously irresponsible, not to mention incompetent. You'll be paid through last week and under the circumstances, consider yourself fortunate. I haven't had the time to look the place over for real damage, yet. Just pack your things and get out and remember, if you're tempted to leave with more than you came with, that the law division of HS Engineering has an exceedingly long reach."

Ivy fell back under the scathing attack, all the more effective for its unemotional delivery. Shock faded, however, to be replaced by a rising anger that was indicated by the flush in her cheeks and the glint in her eyes.

"Now just a minute, there! I admit you have some slight reason for dissatis—"

"Slight!" he exclaimed incredulously.

"Don't interrupt me! You had your say, now I'm going to have mine! All right, so the house may not be what you might call orderly. . . ."

"Don't put ideas in my head," he sneered disparagingly.

As if he had not spoken, Ivy continued, "I'll be the first to admit it's a mess, but there are excuses. . . ."

"There is no possible excuse for what I've just seen! You've obviously had some sort of wild party here, an every night affair, for all I know, unless it's your usual standard of housekeeping."

He was matching her anger and going her one better and Ivy shrunk against the hall table, noticing with dismay a half-eaten ham biscuit nestled among the shattered chrysanthemum petals.

"Either way," the man continued implacably, "you can't expect me to condone such behavior. You're either too immature or too irresponsible to handle such a position and there's only one reason I can come up with for Hooper to have installed you here." His eyes made an insulting survey of her person again. "And that's even *more* unflattering. At any rate, I don't want you on my property a minute longer than necessary, understand?"

Stunned, Ivy backed toward the stairway. As she reached the bottom step, stumbling slightly, she looked at him again, her eyes enormous shimmering pools. "Won't you at least let me explain?" she pleaded.

"There *is* no explanation! I suppose you've spread yourself around up there, haven't you? Hooper probably told you no one from HS ever checked up on the place and the two of you thought you could play house in perfect safety."

He moved relentlessly forward and Ivy backed unsteadily up the stairs, wondering how she could combat such vindictive unfairness.

"It's almost a shame to break up such a perfect setup. It probably won't be easy to find as cozy a nest for your purposes." The anger suddenly seemed to drain away, leaving him tired and bitter.

"I don't know who you are, but you're wrong about . . . about all this," Ivy insisted, gesturing help-

lessly around her. "And furthermore, you've absolutely no right to insinuate such hateful things."

"I have every right," he barked, standing below her
with his well-shod feet apart, his hands on his lean hips
as if he owned the place. "My name, for your information, is Hunter Smith. This is solely my property and as
of now, you're trespassing!"

"And you're a . . . a . . . !"

"Careful. You're much too young to be using the
kind of language you're thinking," Hunter Smith
warned, a glint in his eye that in anyone else might be
mistaken for amusement.

Spinning around, Ivy flew upstairs, slamming her
bedroom door after her, to fling herself against it. It
didn't help to know she looked far younger than her
age and utterly without pride or dignity.

Nothing helped now! Darn the man for dropping in
unannounced! If only he had come yesterday when
everything was clean and sparkling . . . if only she
hadn't given in to Finley's persuasion against her better
judgment . . . if only . . .

She flattened her damp palms against the cool
painted wood and made an effort to calm her breathing. Spread herself around, indeed, she thought dole-
fully, looking about her at the tiny room with its odd
assortment of cast-off furniture. It had been a point of
honor with her to take the poorest room, leaving all the
others aired and ready for her absentee employer. She
had spent just one night in her lovely old room with its
gray-green, rose, and white decorations, before decid-
ing it was necessary to impress on herself the change in
her circumstances.

No longer the daughter of the house . . . the grand-
daughter, to be more precise, she had deliberately
reminded herself that she was only the caretaker, a paid
employee who, while she might occasionally entertain a
few friends on her employer's premises, must keep in
mind that Rougemont was not hers to take liberties
with.

Well, so much for smug self-righteousness! She threw her clothes into her two suitcases, thanking her good fortune that she had not, as he accused her, spread herself around. Except for her silver-working tools out in the shed, which Fin could collect for her later, she could be out of here in twenty minutes and good riddance!

She heard his firm, angry sounding steps echoing down the hall as if stamping it with his brand and she knew instinctively that Rougemont would never be the same again.

On the point of stepping into her jeans, she changed her mind and pulled out a wool jersey dress in a lovely shade of wood violet. Let him see that she was no mere fly-by-night kid! She shimmied into a pair of panty hose and jammed her feet into brown suede pumps before reaching for her hairbrush. Sparks fairly flew as she took out her feelings on her thick, unruly mop and she made several false starts before her trembling fingers finally managed to pile it on top of her head in some semblance of order.

She took time to smooth on a thin film of makeup, finishing it off with a brave dash of cherry lip gloss. Even so, she was downstairs in twenty-five minutes, her coat over her arm and her two suitcases beside her.

It was only then that she remembered the most immediate problem facing her: transportation. Fin had handed her the keys to the ancient jeep along with those to the house when she had first taken the job. It had seemed almost funny at the time, for she had used those same keys for years. Only now, the jeep went with the job and the job had gone and the only thing remaining was Ivy, herself, and she hadn't the slightest idea how she was going to leave.

She was still grappling with the problem when she heard a door open down the hall and turning, she frowned at the man who appeared in the doorway, almost filling it with his height and the width of his shoulders. Before she could brace herself to speak up about her lack of transportation, he gestured abruptly for her to enter the library. In the few short moments it took her to reach him, Ivy had the uncomfortable idea he had taken inventory of every stitch she had on and could probably tell to within a few dollars just how much money she had in her purse.

"Mr. Smith, I . . ."

"Miss whatever your name is, come in here for a minute."

They both spoke at once and Hunter Smith won out through sheer force of personality. He nodded to a chair, the most uncomfortable in the room, then seated himself behind her grandfather's massive walnut desk. If he hoped to impress her with his authority, Ivy could have told him that the desk was not necessary; he would have commanded attention at a summit conference!

"What *is* your name, by the way?"

"Ivy de Coursey, Mr. Smith," she stated firmly, belying the trembling of her knees. Resolutely, she pressed her feet more firmly against the worn Aubusson and stiffened her spine.

"Hmmmm. De Coursey. Any relation to the previous owners?"

"Yes."

"Would you care to elaborate?"

"Not really," she answered resentfully. "What difference does it make?"

"Nevertheless, I think you'd better explain what you're doing here masquerading as a housekeeper," he insisted.

Briefly, she told him how she had come to accept the job, leaving out the fact that she had left her previous position in rather too great haste for her own good, and that she had come back to Rougemont to be nearer Finley. She had an idea he suspected that much, if not more.

"What was the party in aid of, or was it simply nightly entertainment? There's not much going on out here in the country, is there?" His tone left her in no doubt as to his opinion of her and she lifted her chin and resolved to bite off her tongue before she'd dignify his accusations with an answer.

They weren't even accusations, which was even worse . . . just hateful insinuations! Well, what did she care? She'd be out of here in no more time than it took to collect her pay and she'd never have to see him' again.

"It was a birthday party, if you must know. My friend celebrated most of his birthdays here when he was a boy and I saw no harm in giving him a party, since there was no one here to mind," she told him defensively. Actually, it had been Fin who insisted and he who had provided everything but the place, but Hunter Smith didn't have to know that.

His silence was unnerving, particularly as he kept on staring at her as if waiting for her to confess to some really heinous crime. She fidgeted, determined to defy him, but her nerves got the better of her.

"Well, it didn't really do any permanent damage," she blurted out, "and anyway, you had no business showing up that way with no warning at all!"

"Oh, so it's my fault, is it?"

"I didn't say that! I accept full responsibility for . . . for the mess we made, but I don't see how you can expect me to have everything all ready for you when you don't even have the decency to call first!"

"If you'd bothered to report an out-of-order phone, you might have saved yourself a good bit of grief," he told her bitingly, his hard, sensuous lips twisted in what might have passed for a smile had it not been for the bleak coldness of his eyes.

"Well, I was going to report it first thing this morning."

"You were fast asleep first, middle, and last thing this morning," he reminded her, "but as long as you admit your behavior was reprehensible I think we might find a way to make partial amends."

"You mean . . . I'm not fired?" Ivy faltered in bewilderment.

"I didn't say that." He paused, letting her run through the gamut of possibilities as he read each succeeding emotion on her open face. At last, leaning forward to place his arms on the top of the desk, well-shaped hands making fists before him, he spoke. "I don't see why I should have the bother of locating someone else to clean up after you. Let's just say I'm allowing you to work out your notice before you go. There are seven days left in the month, so we'll say a week's notice. You stay on and clean the place thoroughly, leaving it in first-class condition, and you'll receive your salary through the end of the month, fair enough?"

"What about a letter of recommendation?" she ventured timidly.

He tipped back his chair in exasperation, emphasizing the splendid chest beneath the sober waistcoat. "Do you honestly expect me to recommend you as a housekeeper after this . . . this debacle?" he asked disbelievingly.

"Well, I'm really not a housekeeper, I'm a secretary, but I don't happen to have any reference for that, either, and with the job market as it is, I don't have much of a chance of finding anything right away." Immediately she hated herself for her hat-in-hand approach. It happened to be true, but she could have kicked herself for asking favors of this infuriating being!

"Oh, come on, now, Miss de Coursey, you want me to recommend you for a service that I haven't even sampled? The very fact that you're without references indicates that your ability as a secretary is on a par with your housekeeping. You'll just have to fall back on something else, won't you? Or some*one* else."

"Mr. Smith!" Ivy jumped to her feet, eyes blazing.

"All right, Miss de Coursey, cool down. A girl has to make a living, I suppose." He sounded suddenly tired of the whole subject and Ivy's anger subsided, to be replaced with a sort of empty despair. He certainly thought the worst of her; she'd better settle for a paycheck and count her blessings.

Torn between frustration and relief, she agreed to stay on until the end of the week. Somehow, this affair was not turning out to suit her, whether she stayed or left, and for the life of her, she couldn't put her finger on quite why. It was enough, she supposed, that she was no longer faced with the immediate prospect of having to find work, a place to stay, and a means of reaching them both.

"Well, go on, what are you waiting for? It's now," he shot a pristine cuff and examined a thin gold watch that glinted among the dark hairs on his wrist, "three minutes to twelve. That just gives you time to clear away enough trash in the kitchen to fix lunch." He looked at her suspiciously. "You *can* cook, I suppose. Not even a brash opportunist like Hooper would send out a complete idiot to handle this job."

"Yes, Mr. Smith, I *can* cook!" Ivy snapped, standing at attention. "If that's all, sir, I'll get started." Her hair-trigger temper was threatening again and it was a luxury she could ill afford. She had reached the door and had her hand on the knob when his voice stopped her.

"Oh, and get those bags out of the hall before one of us trips and breaks a leg. I don't care for things out of their proper places. Move out of whatever room you've been using and into whatever passes for servants' quarters and get the master bedroom ready for me. I put your young man's things out in the hall, by the way. I assume the initials on the toilet case stand for Finley Hooper?"

There was no mistaking the sneer in his voice and Ivy turned away to hide the painful color that stained her face. Of *course* Finley had left his things last night. He had been so dazzled it was a wonder he even remembered where he lived! Trust this outrageous person to snoop around before she even had time to retrieve them.

"I'll go on using the room I've been using at the back of the second floor, sir, if that's all right. The one our old housekeeper used is full of trunks and boxes," she informed him stiffly. "The master bedroom is perfectly ready, sir. It was only . . ."

"Look at me when you speak to me, and stop sirring me every other breath!"

"Yes, sir, Mr. Smith. Will that be all now, Mr. Smith?"

He uttered something extremely unpleasant under his breath and Ivy closed the door softly behind her. There might be a time to clarify the position between her and Finley, but this was definitely not it!

At the foot of the stairs, a suitcase in each hand, she sighed. Had she won or had she lost? Darned if she knew which.

Chapter Two

By the time the sun had dipped below the trees along the riverbank, Ivy could survey her domain with some degree of satisfaction. She had been terribly self-conscious at first, for Hunter Smith had watched her until in frustration she had turned on him and demanded to know whether or not he trusted her.

"If you don't, you know, you can just find someone else to work for you! I can't work with you peeping around the door trying to catch me stuffing my pockets with silverware!"

That might not have been precisely fair, for there was nothing at all furtive in the way he watched her. After going off on his own for a while, he would come back and drop into a chair in whatever room she was working on and stare at her until she could almost feel the skin on her back burning.

"Sorry. I didn't mean to make you uncomfortable."

There was certainly nothing at all uncomfortable in

the way *he* made himself at home, sprawling out in the largest chair with his long, muscular legs stretched out in front of him like some satiated, sun-warmed lion.

"Well, you do!" Ivy persisted. "If I'd been planning to take anything I'd have done it before now. I've been here by myself almost four months, you know!"

"That long," he mused. "Of course, as you well know, I wouldn't have the slightest idea of what was missing without the inventory sheets, and I'm sure your friend, Hooper, retained copies. What a perfect setup."

With a gasp, Ivy stared at him, her fury doubled by the smug, well-dressed attitude he presented with his waistcoat open, his too conservative tie loosened and his bench-made shoes crossed casually before him. Feeling smaller than ever in her shabby work clothes, she threw down her trash bag and duster and marched to the door. This sort of thing she could do without. No job was that important!

"Come back."

She ignored him. In this mood she could walk all the way to Wilkesboro with both suitcases and her box of tools, to boot!

Swift, silent strides brought him to her side and he ringed her wrist with a deceptively gentle manacle.

"You have absolutely no right to say such things to me," she flared, furious at him, even more furious at the tears that swam so blindingly in her eyes.

"You're right, Miss de Coursey, and I apologize."

Her tongue all primed for another tirade, Ivy was thrown off balance by the obvious sincerity of his apology and could only stare at him, seeing a blurred vision of tanned planes and angles that came together in a devastatingly attractive manner.

"Look, I'm really sorry. That was uncalled for, even if your housekeeping does leave something to be desired."

"My housekeeping is perfectly adequate," Ivy defended, tugging against his grip. She was uncomfortably aware of the sensation caused by his hand on her bare flesh.

"After looking over the rest of the house, I'll concede the point. The areas not invaded by your *soi-disant* friends are in perfect order, but you will admit, last night's celebration was an unfortunate thing."

"Unfortunately timed, at least," she muttered under her breath, breaking his grip on her arm at last.

"I have business that will keep me tied up for an hour. Shall we say dinner at seven? No need to prepare anything elaborate. From the looks of the kitchen we could hibernate on the leftovers."

Well, that was a blessing! If he had demanded a full-course meal, he would have gone hungry, for her supplies were carefully geared for one.

Eyeing him suspiciously, she turned away. He seemed all bland friendliness at the moment, but she didn't trust him one bit! He was an ice-capped volcano that could erupt anytime!

The dining-room furniture was still piled at one end so she served him in the breakfast room. It was a pity, for he was just the sort to reign in solitary splendor at the head of an enormous table.

"Join me," he ordered peremptorily, but Ivy declined on the grounds that she had already eaten. She hadn't, of course, but she couldn't have swallowed a bite across from that forbidding countenance.

She put the dishes in to soak and opened the back door to gaze out at the night-shrouded mountains. For some reason, she needed the stability they promised tonight. Her universe seemed to have tilted slightly and she was not certain she could keep her balance.

"Ivy, would you mind sparing me a few minutes in the library?" He spoke from immediately behind her and Ivy started, for she had not even heard him approach.

"Now?" she asked doubtfully.

"When you're finished with your work," he answered

quietly. In the dim back-lighting from the bare kitchen bulb, he looked older than he had this morning.

Ten minutes later she rapped on the library door, nervous and more tired than she would have liked to admit from the heavy day's activity.

"Come in, Ivy," he invited, his voice sounding slightly muffled. He was kneading the muscles at the back of his neck and his face had that vulnerable look of having just been rubbed.

He gestured to a chair, more comfortable than the one she had been offered for the earlier interview, and she sat for more than a minute before he began to speak.

The few minutes he had requested lengthened into almost an hour as Hunter Smith elicited from her every detail concerning Rougemont, its grounds and out-buildings, the nearest towns, their population, the amount of traffic that found its way as far as Rouge-mont, and the available utilities. Ivy answered him readily, for there was nothing personal about any of his questions. Anyone might think he was looking for a hideout from the law, from the way he was quizzing her about visitors in the area.

Under the somnolent ticking of the old Seth Thomas and the various creakings as the house adjusted itself against the oncoming night, Ivy relaxed and tucked one foot up under her, swinging the other idly. "Do you usually buy places like Rougemont without even look-ing them over first?" she dared ask after they had discussed the size and the classic Victorian architecture of the place.

"No, not as a rule, but then, there aren't too many places like Rougemont, are there?" He grinned and the years fell away until Ivy decided he couldn't be more than thirty-five. She also decided to be on her guard against such blatant magnetism. Hunter Smith in a friendly mood was something to behold.

"I've been in Germany and Japan for the past two months and before that, the Netherlands, so this is really the first chance I've had to look the place over since the details were settled."

Ivy refrained from mentioning that he had owned the place for the better part of a year. "What do you think?" she asked instead.

"It's suitable, I believe," he declared obliquely.

"Suitable for what?"

The shutters came down at once, closing out the warmth that had begun to glow in his eyes. "Suitable for my purposes," he told her curtly. "And now I suggest you turn in early. You haven't made much of a dent in all the work to be done and unless you're prepared to get up at a reasonably early hour for a change, you'll still be at it a month from now."

Stung, Ivy struggled to her feet, not helped by the pins and needles that coursed through the one she had been sitting on. "I am not in the habit of sleeping late, sir," she choked. "What time would you like breakfast served?"

"Seven-thirty would be fine and I'd like a pot of coffee and no conversation, served in here, please."

"Coffee alone is not . . ."

"Miss de Coursey!"

"Yes, sir. Good night, sir!" She fled, flags of color flying in her cheeks.

The week went by without incident, surprisingly enough, and Ivy worked diligently, determined to leave Rougemont in absolutely flawless condition. She would have tackled the garden if she had thought there was any chance of making a dent in it, but years of neglect had taken their toll and in all honesty, Ivy admitted she preferred it this way. The shade of the pines, sycamores, and oaks kept undergrowth to a minimum near the house. She could wander endlessly through the carpet of leaves, searching out the wild blueberries, delighting in small patches of Quaker ladies and dogtooth violets. Ground cedar trailed here and there and in a protected corner, her grandmother's old-fashioned cane roses made havoc of the mounds of chrysanthemums and iris.

Finley didn't call and Ivy wondered if he was spending much time with Micki MacNeely. Something had changed between Finley and herself; she sensed this without even being around him, and if she cried a few tears into her pillow at night, then it was no one's business but her own. Her daylight hours, however, had best be concerned with the fact that soon she would be leaving Rougemont for good. A paycheck, while adequate, would not allow for much dragging of the feet when it came to finding another job and a place to stay. She didn't want to return to Charlotte, but there was Winston-Salem, or even Asheville. With the ski season gearing up she might find something at Beech or Sugar Mountain or at Seven Devils.

On Friday morning she was automatically feeding the rings of the heavy velvet draperies onto the rod when she heard the phone ringing in the library. Knowing Hunter was there, busy as usual with the endless papers that bulged the sides of his briefcase, she went on with what she was doing.

She heard the low rumble of his voice as he answered it and pictured him tipping back his chair, arms stretched back behind his head with his shirt unbuttoned to reveal the dark thatch on his chest. She had seen him relax in just that way each time she interrupted him with coffee and not even to herself had she admitted how disturbing she found him.

"It's for you, Ivy," he called through the doorway.

Ivy looked over her shoulder and almost overbalanced on the ladder as she held up one end of the rod toward the bracket.

"Watch it. . . . Don't move until I grab that thing." He was beside her in an instant, easily reaching the bracket she could manage only from the ladder. "Down you go, now . . . easy, I've got you." He steadied her with a solid grip on her arm and as she reached the floor, she brushed against him.

Hurriedly, she pulled away and dashed for the phone. It would have to be Finley.

It was. "Ivy? Long time no see."

She took a deep breath to steady herself before answering. "Hello, Finley. How are you?"

"Busy, gal, busy! Working day and night to clear my desk before the end of the year. Can't afford to leave any loose ends, you know, in case I might need a favor sometime. Look, Ive, I'm sorry I had to leave you with all the mess. I understand you have company out there now. That who answered the phone?"

"If you mean Mr. Smith, yes. How did you find out?"

"He took the bread right out of my mouth, if you must know. Left word at the office that from now on he'd deal with the Rougemont staff in person. What staff? Do you have anyone else out there?"

"I'm it. At least, temporarily." She remembered the open door and lowered her voice. "Fin, it was dreadful! You really left me in the lurch and *he* turned up bright and early on Saturday morning before I even had a chance to empty an ashtray. I'm lucky to have escaped with my skin in one piece!"

"Oh, that's tough, honey, but it sounds as if you survived. Look, what I called about . . . I left some things out there. Did you find them?"

"Oh, did I ever! Mr. Smith found them in his bedroom and before I even knew they were there he had it all figured out."

"You and me, you mean?" Finley hooted. "That's ridiculous!"

Piqued, Ivy held back the retort that rose to her lips. What was so ridiculous about it? He was a man and she was a woman and they were both of age.

After a brief silence Finley asked her if she'd mind bringing his things to him. "I'll treat you to a dinner if you'll do it, Ive. I can't get away from the office until late, but you could bring the things and meet me and we'd take my car. How about it?"

"What about Micki?" she blurted out in spite of herself.

"Oh, she's gone back to Orlando for a week or so. Why?"

Why, indeed? Finley's answer settled something in Ivy's mind, but she agreed to meet him if her employer gave her time off.

After hanging up the phone she stood there for several minutes. Had there been the slightest bit of embarrassment in Fin's voice when he told her Micki was out of town? Funny that he couldn't find time for even a call until now. Well, one thing was certain: she had no notion of ever letting him know of her own feelings. She had far too much pride for that!

"Mr. Smith," she broached the subject as soon as she reentered the library, "may I have the evening off?"

"Hooper?"

"Yes, sir," she answered tightly, resenting his inquisitiveness.

"Is he coming out here to see you?"

"No, sir, I'm driving in to Wilkesboro to meet him after work. That is, if I may use the jeep."

"Why doesn't he pick you up here? It's no sort of country for a girl alone to be driving in at night."

"It's my country, sir, and I don't mind."

"How long does it take to get to his office?"

"Forty-five minutes in the jeep." She knew Hunter Smith drove a Jensen Interceptor and she had an idea he'd make the trip in much less time.

He was frowning, tugging at his lower lip the way he did when he was deep in thought. "All right." He nodded. "You may go if you promise me to be back at a reasonable hour and to call me as soon as you get back in the house."

"Wha-a-at?" Not even her grandfather, when she was a teenager, had been so strict.

"You heard me. I have to go to Atlanta tonight and there won't be anyone here to know or care whether or not you get home safely, so I insist you call me."

"But that's ridiculous! I've lived here all by myself for months and before that I was on my own in Charlotte. I don't have to answer to you for what I do!" she cried in dismay.

"It's about time someone else took a hand in your welfare, then, young lady, and while you're working for me, you'll answer to me, is that clear?" He pulled out a flat, small case and extracted a card. "Here," handing it to her, "call the second number tonight, the other if you need me during the day."

Reluctantly, she took it and slipped it into her pocket, still not sure she'd use it.

"Use it!" he barked, causing her to jump and stare at him suspiciously.

"Please," he added more gently, undermining her resolution to defy him. "That is unless you were planning to spend the night with him."

That did it! She'd never call him! "No, sir, I was not, nor have I ever!" she cried angrily.

One half of the draperies were hanging. Ivy ignored the other panel; she had to get away or she'd strangle the man. She marched stiffly from the room and managed to keep busy in the kitchen until she heard him go into the library and slam the door.

By five o'clock, she was dressed and ready to go. It was much too early, but she didn't dare risk another run-in with Hunter Smith. On the point of collecting the keys from the nail beside the kitchen door, she remembered something that had slipped her mind entirely; her week was up Sunday and if Hunter was leaving tonight, it was quite possible that he would not be back by then. She badly needed that final paycheck, and if she could force herself to pretend a meekness she was far from feeling, she just might wangle a letter of recommendation, too, in spite of his earlier refusal. It would go a long way toward helping her secure another position, for she was not foolish enough to ignore the weight a name like Hunter Smith would carry.

Grabbing her coat from the hall closet, she was struggling into it when the door to the library opened and the man came striding toward her.

"Ivy, before you go, spare me a minute, would you?" he demanded distractedly. His sleeves were rolled up, his shirt opened halfway to his belt, and his hair looked as if he had been running his hands through it.

Ivy went on struggling with her sleeves. As usual when she was in a hurry, her fists jammed in the ripped place in the lining. Wouldn't you just know!

Hunter reached out and lifted the coat away from her shoulders, enabling her to pull out her arms and start again, and when she was done, instead of stepping away, he allowed his hands to move to the turned-up collar and smooth it, back to front. His hands brushed against her throat and Ivy stepped back quickly, her eyes flying up with a wary look.

"You must be in a hurry," he commented, a glint of amusement lighting his face.

"I am," she replied breathlessly.

"What time are you meeting him?"

Her mind struggled with an answer to his point-blank question and he evidently read her hesitation with ease, for he only grinned at her, causing her to color furiously. Darn the man for putting her out of countenance so easily!

"May I go now?" she asked desperately, forgetting her reason for needing to see him.

"Just one thing. I may not be here until Sunday night and I don't want you leaving before I get back. I owe you a month's salary, remember?"

"May I have it now?" she dared.

"If you insist. I'm leaving cash in the lower left desk drawer and I'd like you to restock the freezer while I'm gone. Use it for anything else you need. I've called about having a load of gravel delivered for the driveway, but it won't come until next week sometime and I should be back by then, barring unforeseen incidents."

"But I'll be gone by then."

"I'd like you to stay, Ivy," he insisted calmly. "I may be bringing back guests with me and I don't want to have to try to find someone new to break in at a time like that. Besides, you're familiar with the place and you like it, don't you?"

"I love it," she said simply, "but that's not the point."

"What is the point?"

"You said I was to work out a week's notice and leave," she insisted, feeling herself on shifting sands. "I'm too young and too incompetent, remember?" It somehow seemed important to get away from Rougemont and this disturbing man whose changing moods were throwing her off balance all too frequently.

"We'll discuss it further when I get back; meanwhile, you'll be here when I return, promise?"

"Oh, all right," she agreed grudgingly.

"Gracious of you." He laughed, then, sobering, "You will call when you get in tonight?"

"If I have to."

"You have to! Don't lose that card and don't forget to call me as soon as you get home."

She might have known his good humor would not last long enough for her to get away. Resentfully, she warned him, "I might be late, you know. Don't blame me if I wake you up at some ungodly hour."

"It had better not be too ungodly. There's not enough traffic on this road late at night for you to be safe. You could have car trouble and be out there all night long."

"How did I ever get through twenty-two years without your kind supervision?" she flung at him, irritated beyond discretion.

"I'm not at all sure you did," he grinned, unexpectedly. "I could have sworn you weren't out of your teens yet."

Dinner was not an unqualified success. Ivy found herself unable to put her last interview with Hunter Smith from her mind. How long was he expecting her to remain? Who were the guests he was bringing back? Her attention wandered as she visualized his ruggedly handsome face, the deep lines somehow adding to the masculine appeal, and she wondered how many women had felt that physical blow to the senses when his stern features relaxed into a warm, crinkly smile. There must be many, for his sort of subtle sexuality would attract any woman. It was a good thing she herself was in love with Finley or she might find herself falling under his spell, too.

"What's with you, anyhow? I might as well be talking in Swahili the past half hour for all the attention you've paid," Finley complained.

Ashamed of her wandering attention, Ivy reached across the table and squeezed his hand. "Try your Swahili on me and we'll see," she teased him.

"I was telling you about what Sam said last week. His man in Orlando has been running the agency single-handedly, but it's getting too big and so I'm going in as a full partner. Wilmouth-Hooper, how does that sound?"

"Why not Hooper-Wilmouth?"

"That'll come, don't worry." Finley's perfect teeth flashed in a broad smile. "Sam says give it a year, then he'll send Wilmouth on to open up a branch and I can have the Orlando office. Micki says I'll love Orlando. She says . . ."

He was off again and through her own wandering thoughts, Ivy was dimly aware of Micki's name popping in and out of his monologue. It didn't bother her enough to recall her from the nebulous area of her own imagination.

"You want dessert?" Finley asked impatiently. "I promised to call Micki at ten. At least we have this sort of agreement," he amended.

"Sure. I mean, no dessert. I have some apples in the jeep to munch on to keep me awake."

"You must have been going to bed with the hens if you're worried about falling asleep at this hour."

"As a matter of fact, I have, but anyway, how was I to know I'd be dismissed so early?"

Finley had the grace to look slightly ashamed as Ivy followed him out to his late-model Buick. They drove back to his office in five minutes and she said good night absently and climbed up into her drafty old jeep. She *was* used to going to bed early, but not necessarily to sleep. After the first few evenings of watching Hunter go through his papers, make endless notes and reshuffle letters impatiently, she decided it would be better for her to remain up in her room. There were books she had gotten from the library that were already overdue and she had not even opened them. Besides, there was something entirely too intimate about sitting around the living room after dinner with Hunter in the library, only a few feet away. She was more conscious of how alone they were all the time. It was beginning to worry her. After the Alan Lancing fiasco and the silly, abortive thing with Finley, the last thing she needed was a wild infatuation!

It was as Ivy was gearing down to negotiate the hill that the idea popped into her head: what if his guest were a wife? There was no reason to believe he wasn't married. There was no indication that he was, either, but that meant nothing. Not all married men wore rings and certainly not all of them *acted* married. She wondered what his wife would be like.

Her spirits seemed to drag as she waded through the weeds from the lean-to where the jeep was kept, to the back door. She turned up the thermostat, tossed her coat at the hall table, and went directly to the library. May as well get it over, she told herself, trying to pretend she wasn't dying to hear his voice again. She couldn't remember when Rougemont had seemed so empty!

The phone rang four times and she was beginning to have visions of a sleepy, disgruntled Hunter barking at her from Atlanta.

"Hello."

The woman's voice, soft and husky, startled her and she could not speak for a minute.

"Hello. Who is this, please?" it repeated, impatience thinning out some of the attractive huskiness.

"Is Mr. Hunter Smith there, please? This is Ivy de Coursey," she managed at last.

"Hunt, it's for you." The woman spoke away from the phone and within a minute, Hunter came on the line.

"Ivy? You in for the night? Good."

"You asked me to call," she reminded him defensively.

"That's right, I did. All locked up now?"

"Not yet."

"Then go do it and report back," he ordered.

"Oh, all right!"

The kitchen, vast and shadowy, gave her an uncomfortably empty feeling as she flipped the night latch. She was usually fairly casual about such things for there had never been any trouble of that sort out here in the country. Still, she had to realize that Rougemont was no longer hers to expose to risks.

"Done," she reported breathlessly.

"Fine. Take care of yourself and don't climb that ladder while I'm gone. The rungs are all but rotted off."

"Yes, sir, will that be all, sir?"

He laughed and the low sound, traveling over hundreds of miles, had a most peculiar effect in the region of her spine.

"Yes, Ivy, that will be all. Surely from this distance you don't need all those sirs between us. Now, tuck yourself up like a good girl and I'll see you sometime on Sunday. Good night."

"Good night . . . sir," she repeated dutifully. Her voice, on that last word, had sunk to a whisper. How did he know she used the sirs as a barrier against him? She hadn't even known it herself until he said that. More important, who was the woman who answered his phone so late at night?

It could only be a wife, she thought. The words Finley had used so long ago to describe the president of HS Engineering came back to her and she conceded with a disconcerting degree of dismay that there could be any number of women who might answer his phone late at night.

She lay awake long after the clock had announced the morning hours puzzling over her reactions to a man she had known only a week.

Saturday morning Ivy awoke to see the last few stubborn sycamore leaves flashing gold against a cobalt sky. She lay there steeling herself for the chilly dash across the room to slam her window shut and in those few minutes she decided to take the day off.

When the cat's away, she told herself. Maybe last night's taste of freedom had gone to her head. At any rate, there was nothing much to do in the house, for she had long since cleared away any signs of the party.

She spent the day afield, following familiar wooded gullies, climbing a group of oddly shaped rocks where she had played as a child and reveling in the fragrant, richly colored quietness.

Leaning against the few remaining planks of an old boat house, she ate a ham biscuit and two speckled pears and then napped for an hour in the late-afternoon sun.

Making her way home through the amber-lighted fields, she slowed her steps, searching for arrowheads as she had done each year after the crops were in. It had been a favorite pastime for both her and Fin-

ley when they were younger and each year she
thought there would be no more, but the flooding river
and the constant rains that washed down the topsoil
from the surrounding hills uncovered a few more each
year.

This time she picked up two large broken flints and a
perfect quartz birdpoint, thrilling to the idea that no
hands had touched them since brown fingers had fixed
them to a shaft hundreds of years before.

Outside the back door, she picked the beggar's-lice
from her jeans and slipped off her muddy sneakers,
breathing deeply of the dry, sweet fragrance of the
withered garden. It had always been one of her favorite
things about Rougemont, the scent of growing things,
of earth and wax and good things cooking.

Rougemont. It was so much a part of her that it
had torn the heart from her to have to leave it after
her grandfather had died. Could she do it again? Perhaps she should consider staying on. The idea of being
close to Finley no longer held the magic it once did,
but she still had Rougemont. She refused to think
of the subtle changes that had come over the old house
since the new man took up residence, but her whole
body was aware of a sense of excitement that filled the
rooms, replacing the earlier feeling of peace and con-
tentment.

Television held no attractions for her that night.
After wandering restlessly from room to room, she
gave up and decided to shampoo her hair and have an
early night.

She lathered and rinsed, lathered and rinsed again.
Then with her hair in a towel, she patted her body dry,
studying her image almost abstractedly in the mirror as
she did.

For no reason, a fiery blush warmed her skin and she
hastily reached for her pajamas, buttoning the peach-
colored top close to her throat before padding down the
back stairs to warm a pan of milk. Beside her bed was a
reissue of an Inglis Fletcher novel that should keep her

entertained until sleep claimed her. Too many restless nights lately had made her wary of still another, but after a whole day spent outdoors, she should have no trouble.

An hour later, with two pages read, Ivy gave up and went back downstairs. She put on another pan of milk to heat and wandered into the living room to stir up the banked fire. Its flickering light might have a hypnotic effect on her. The radio produced a rather ponderous symphony to which she listened just long enough to decide she was not in the mood for it, but a flick of the dial tuned in the sweet strains of a song Ivy had always thought too romantic. Tonight it seemed just the thing.

Settling herself on the sofa with a stool pulled alongside to hold her mug of milk, she pulled the afghan over her body and closed her eyes, willing herself to think of black velvet.

Something nibbled away at the edges of her consciousness and she stirred, blinking warily in the darkness. There it was again, a sound as if someone— or something—were scratching at the front door. Could it be one of Mattie's stray dogs? There had once been a constant stream of them at the back door and one just might have turned up here, looking for a handout.

It came again, this time followed by a sharp click and the sighing of the hinges.

Someone had opened that door!

Heavy, slow footsteps crossed the hall and seemed to hesitate and a chill feathered across Ivy's neck. She had locked that door. She might have been careless in the past, but not since Hunter Smith had been in residence.

There was a thud, as if something heavy had dropped to the floor, and silently, with no conscious thought except to protect Rougemont against whoever was breaking in in the middle of the night, she eased back the afghan and swung her feet to the floor. Unconsciously holding her breath, she took a step, tripped on the stool, and fell flat on her face.

The lights that flashed in her head were far more impressive than the sudden incandescence that was almost swallowed up by the dark oak paneling.

"For heaven's sake, are you all right?"

Ungentle hands were helping her to a sitting position and she blinked up at the dark face above her, breathing in the cold night air and the scent of good woolens that clung to him.

"Why didn't you tell me it was you?" she demanded angrily.

"How was I to know you were waiting here in the dark to tackle me as soon as I came through the door?"

"I was not waiting for you! I didn't even know you were coming! You said Sunday!"

"Do I have to make reservations to come home? And technically it is Sunday!"

She could see more clearly now and he looked dreadful, the lines etched more deeply than ever in his lean cheeks.

Attempting to get up, she was unable to stifle a sound that was part gasp, part groan, and instantly his hands were on her shoulders, their warmth burning through her thin nylon top.

"Did you hurt something? Here, let me help you up off the floor, at least."

He still sounded anything *but* sympathetic and Ivy brushed away his hands, struggling to her feet, barely avoiding the shards of her mug beside the overturned stool. Head still reeling, she lowered herself gingerly onto the sofa.

"Looks as if you might be sporting a black eye for a few days," Hunter commented with what Ivy took to be satisfaction. He dropped heavily down beside her and she inched away, frowning at him and then wincing as the movement brought pain.

"I must have landed on my cheekbone, if that's possible," she grumbled. Testing her limbs, she found nothing seriously wrong, but when she touched the area below her left eye her fingers encountered a grazed place and she caught her breath.

"Here, let me see," Hunter murmured, so close suddenly that she could feel the warmth of his breath as it played across her face. He cupped her chin and angled it toward the light and Ivy was unable to look away from the brooding darkness of his face. She was acutely conscious of the texture of his skin and of the clean male smell of him and when his own shadowed eyes strayed to engage hers, she could not break away.

There was all the time in the world to avoid what happened next, but Ivy was hopelessly entangled. She watched as his face came closer, his eyes never losing contact with her own, until suddenly everything went out of focus and there was nothing but feeling, a wild spiral of expectancy as his mouth closed softly over hers. Of their own volition, her hands fluttered up to touch his face, his hair, and then she was holding him closer, closer, and he was pressing her back against the cushions with the weight of his urgent body. His hard mouth beguiled her lips apart with a hot, sweet magic and drank its fill even as his hands worked a magic all their own over her body.

She hardly knew when the thin stuff of her top slithered from her shoulders, but her breath caught in an agonizing gasp as his seeking lips found the swollen peak of her breast.

Faint alarms began sounding in her inner mind and she became aware of the rough surging of his heart against the rapid counterpoint of her own and then he was lifting her in his arms, murmuring words that barely pierced the curious floating sense of detatchment that swallowed her up.

"What are you doing? Where are you taking me?" she managed to whisper, barely hearing the sound of her own voice over the rush of her pulses.

"Where do you think?"

His lips flickered over her upturned face, brushing featherlike kisses across her eyelids, sliding sensuously across her cheek to the corner of her mouth. As his tongue began to probe gently, Ivy began to struggle.

"No, please . . . we can't!"

They were halfway up the stairs by then and fear was fast replacing the drugged honey that had flowed through her veins a moment before.

"Please, Hunter," she whispered, burying her face in his warm throat. She was trembling almost uncontrollably.

He stiffened, but continued determinedly until he reached the top of the stairs; then he put her on her feet and caught her as she swayed.

"Ivy?" he asked softly, almost tentatively.

"Oh, what am I doing here? I don't even *like* you," she cried, covering her face with her hands as she pulled herself away from him. She twisted away and ran, hearing him call after her, but panic held her now and she flung herself across the bed, her hands pressed tightly against her ears.

A tiny part of her mind wondered if he would come after her, even as she castigated herself for behaving with such wild abandon. What had she been thinking of? A man she hardly knew, her employer!

She sobbed brokenly into her pillow, hardly aware of the chill that stole over her, and sometime in the night she roused to feel the soft drift of a comforter as it settled gently over her body.

Chapter Three

Troubled dream fragments followed her into wakefulness the next morning and she groped about in her mind for something elusive that stayed just out of reach. The first recollection came as she passed a rough washcloth over her face. Until then she had not even glanced in the mirror, but at the sharp pain, she turned and stared at her reflection.

Mottled. That was the only word she could come up with to describe the way she looked, with her spattering of freckles now augmented by purple shadows beneath her eyes and a matching bruise on her cheekbone.

Oddly enough, she found her appearance reassuring. Surely she had dreamed it all—Hunter's lovemaking and the panic-stricken flight to the safety of her own room? No one could make love to a face like that!

But as she slowly slipped out of her pajamas and stood under a warm shower, the details came back with agonizing clarity.

How on earth could she face the man across the breakfast table and ignore the fact that she had almost ended up in his bed last night? How does one manage such things? Hunter Smith might have the savoir faire required, but Ivy de Coursey was another matter. One thing was certain; his opinion of her couldn't be lower!

Of course, there had been that misunderstanding about Finley from the very beginning, but as she had expected to be gone momentarily, she had done nothing to rectify it. Then, as her time was extended, there seemed no opening into which to drop the information that she was not now, nor had she ever been, Finley's lover.

She dug out her makeup and spread foundation over her face in an effort to cover the shadows and bruises, wincing as she touched her pale cheeks with blusher. Reaching for the violet wool, she stopped, muttered a mild imprecation and grabbed her jeans and a faded peach pullover, instead. For good measure, she scrubbed her face clean of makeup, taking a perverse pleasure in the pain she inflicted on her poor battered cheekbone. It seemed in some small way to atone for her shameless behavior of the night before.

By the time she got downstairs the coffee was perked and there were signs that her employer had made himself a skimpy breakfast. Not that he ever wanted more than toast and coffee and a bit of cheese, and that with his nose in the eternal charts and letters that took up most of his time.

Ivy poured herself a cup of coffee, tasted it and grimaced. It seemed to give her the strength she needed, however, and she put her cup down on the counter, braced her shoulders and marched determinedly off to the library. Never one to shirk an unpleasant duty, she rapped briskly on the door.

Besides, if she stopped to think, she might start running and never stop!

"Come in."

She opened the door cautiously, then began to speak

in a rush with her eyes focused somewhere high on the opposite wall.

"Mr. Smith, if you'll just make out my check, I'd like to get an early start. I can take the jeep as far as Wilkesboro and leave it there to be collected later, if that's all right."

He lifted one sardonic brow and tipped his chair back, playing idly with a gold pen.

"You were going somewhere this morning?"

"Well, yes," she faltered. "It's Sunday, you know."

"Ahhh, Sunday. And you, no doubt, were on your way to church." His eyes dropped slowly, insolently down her body and she wished her jeans did not cling quite so faithfully to her thighs.

"I'm leaving. You said a week, remember? Well, today makes a week."

"I also said I had guests coming and would prefer that you stay, Miss de Coursey. You have my word there won't be a repeat of last night's . . . uh, activities. Charge it up to the fact that you were half asleep, frightened, and disoriented and I hadn't slept for almost twenty hours. Both of us were pretty punchy for one reason or another, so let's forget it, hmmm?"

Ivy bristled. "I'm perfectly willing to forget it, Mr. Smith, and I'm quite certain there won't be a repeat, but all the same, I'd like to leave. It's really not proper, anyway. I mean, just the two of us here alone. This is a conservative area, you know, and . . . well, this sort of thing . . ." She shrugged and felt herself go red. "It's not as if you had . . . had your f-family," she blurted out desperately.

"Quit stammering, Ivy. You're lighted up like a Christmas tree. As to that, I'm sorry I can't produce a family on tap, but perhaps a fiancée would fill the bill."

She stared at him, noticing again how very tired he looked. Of course, lack of sleep . . . and from the sound of the voice on his telephone in Atlanta, he might have missed two nights in a row!

"Your . . . your fiancée will be coming to stay?" she asked hesitantly.

"That's right," he replied blandly, watching every flicker of expression on her face.

Really, did he have to turn the screw? He must know how she was feeling, for in spite of her heated words at the top of the stairs last night, she had left him in no doubt as to the pitiful state of her defences.

"With or without my pay, I'm leaving, Mr. Smith," she declared belligerently. "Your fiancée can look after things for you, can't she?" She felt her eyes begin to sting and turned away in case they began to water.

Hard fingers bit into her shoulders. "Listen here to me, you little firebrand, you gave me your word you'd stay and I intend to hold you to it."

Ivy shrugged her shoulders, trying to escape the dangerous excitement of his touch, and he shook her ruthlessly.

"Ivy!" Then, in a suddenly gentle voice, he continued. "Climb down, girl, you can't walk all the way to Wilkesboro on a day like this and I refuse to let you take the jeep."

Despairingly, she turned to the window, only to stifle a gasp at the sight of a sodden rain that fell heavily, obscuring all but the nearest trees.

The fingers on her shoulders eased up and were now soothing flesh that would probably be blue within hours. "There now, you see? You simply can't march out of here in high dudgeon on a day like this. It would completely kill the effectiveness of your gesture before you had gone ten feet," he informed her with an engaging grin.

In spite of herself, Ivy responded to the lightning change of mood, even as she backed away from the treacherous warmth of his touch. How could anyone be so infuriating one minute and so utterly irresistible the next? She'd better keep on reminding herself, for her own safety, how much she disliked the man.

"I'm well aware of your opinion of me," he said,

reading her mind with disconcerting accuracy, "but I badly need your help at the moment."

"What about getting someone from Atlanta? You threatened to do that when I first came."

"You looked on it as a threat? How revealing," Hunter observed. Then, before she could repudiate the charge, "For reasons I'm not prepared to go into at the moment, I need someone who's familiar with every aspect of Rougemont. You fill the bill, you're on the spot without another position, and despite what you may think, I trust you implicitly. That's important to me."

Astounded, Ivy could only stare at him. Did he know how persuasive such an argument could be? Was he deliberately manipulating her?

"Wow! You really pull out all the stops, don't you? But I still don't see why your fiancée can't take over? You trust her, surely."

Hunter sighed, lifting a hand to his temple, then went on to massage the muscles at the back of his neck in a gesture she had noticed with increasing frequency lately. "Ivy, Evelyn is not officially my fiancée yet. She's a widow with two small children and needs someone to look after her. I've made the offer, but she hasn't yet accepted, or let's say, she's accepted conditionally."

Bewildered, Ivy could only ask, "What do you mean, conditionally?"

"Later, girl. Right now I'm expecting a call from Athens and I don't want to get involved in any long-winded explanations. Not that it's really any of your business, you know." He smiled that oddly endearing smile of his and for once, she didn't take offense at his words. "Look, promise me you'll stay as long as I need you and I'll give you a bonus when you go. Say, five thousand dollars for three months plus a letter of recommendation for whatever position you decide on, how's that?"

"It's far too much!" she told him indignantly. "I

don't need to be bribed! My regular salary and a letter of reference will be enough."

"Fine. A glowing letter it shall be. Now, you'll need to get things ready, I suppose. There'll be another guest, as well as Evelyn's two girls. Nice kids, four and five. Too quiet, perhaps, but here in the country, maybe they'll learn to cut loose a little."

"Is the other one a child, too?"

"Bill? Hardly. Bill Walters and I were at prep school together, although Bill's a few years older than I. He's a good friend as well as being my personal physician. You'll like him."

As she left to go prepare the rooms, she felt her relationship with Hunter slip imperceptibly into another phase. Friendship might be too strong a word; nevertheless, it was disconcerting and far from reassuring to realize what an extraordinarily nice person he could be. Somehow that, along with his stunning physical magnetism, was a greater threat than she had bargained for and Ivy decided it was a good thing his fiancée was coming.

She was halfway to the kitchen when she turned back with an exclamation. "Oh, I forgot!"

"Forgot what?" Hunter called through the open door, sounding now as tired as he had looked.

"The shopping," she admitted shamefacedly. "I went for a long walk yesterday and didn't get back until just before dark and I forgot all about needing to restock."

"Oh, well, it's too late now, I suppose. You'll just have to do the best you can with what's on hand. Evelyn won't be expecting *cordon bleu* and Bill will welcome anything as long as there's plenty of it. The children won't make that much difference."

"I'm sorry, Mr. Smith. I can put together a meal, though. There is one last roast in the freezer and a few jars of home-canned things left."

"What on earth did you live on before I came?"

"Oh . . . bits and pieces. I managed."

"Not very well from what I've noticed. Oil tanks all but empty, firewood almost gone, pantry cleaned out. You must have eaten out a good deal, compliments of Hooper, I suppose. You'd think I wasn't paying you enough to live on."

"I was paid a perfectly adequate salary. Not princely, mind you, but adequate! I didn't overstock on anything because I didn't know you were coming, remember? And since then . . ."

"Since then you've either been on the verge of quitting or being fired, right?" He was still seated behind the desk, but he leaned back now, a crooked smile warming his expression.

"That wasn't what I was going to say, but now that you mention it, I *have* had one foot in the unemployment line for rather a long time," she returned with a tremulous smile of her own.

"Point taken. I've had the oil tank topped off and a load of wood delivered and I thought I might have a go at kindling, myself. I found an ax in the building out beside the jeep shelter. As a matter of interest, how did you plan to keep warm this winter?"

"I'd have closed off most of the house," she told him frankly. "We used to close down a good portion of it, anyway, just to save Mattie's legs as much as anything else."

"Couldn't you do Mattie's running for her?"

"I did do some of it, but for three years my grandmother was bedridden. Mattie kept the house and my grandfather going and I did the nursing."

He seemed almost to forget her presence as his hand slipped behind his neck in the familiar gesture. He had left off his tie and waistcoat the past few days and his clothes were gradually taking on more of a country look, even though they were still the flawlessly tailored slacks and the custom-made shirts.

"Well, we'll see," he said now, coming back with a visible effort. "Right now, you'd better scare up something for a meal tonight and see to those rooms.

Evelyn will want the children in with her, I suppose, or as close as possible. . . . Strange house and all that." He sounded as if he were familiar with the needs of a child in a strange house and for an instant Ivy had the impression that he was remembering something in his own past.

Her attention stumbled back to the present. "Yes, sir."

"Oh, and Ivy, the name is Hunter. Use it," he commanded with a lift of those heavy, straight brows.

"Oh, but I couldn't!"

"Do I have to break down those barriers again?" he threatened softly.

"What do you mean?"

"I think you know," he suggested silkily.

She fled, torn between outrage and amusement. How could he remind her of that! And anyway, what would his fiancée think to hear his housekeeper calling her employer by his given name? An impudent smile trembled on her lips as she hurried up the stairs.

If subconsciously Ivy had drawn up a mental picture of a bereaved woman with two small children, a widow who leaned on Hunter Smith's dominant strength, Evelyn Carlin shattered the image within five minutes of her arrival.

In the first place, she was one of the loveliest women Ivy had ever seen; tall, almost emaciated in her elegant, expensive clothes, her hair swung against a swanlike neck in a shimmering black cloud. Her features were perfect, her complexion flawless, all of which made Ivy more conscious than ever of her own shortcomings.

There were no children in evidence and as Bill Walters, a middle-aged man whom Ivy liked on sight, came staggering in under a heavy burden of luggage, Ivy heard Evelyn explaining to Hunter the absence of the two small girls.

"Oh, darling, I was afraid they'd get on your nerves.

You need peace and quiet at a time like this and you know how awful they can be . . . whining constantly for attention just when you settle down for a cozy drink. Grace is taking care of them. I told her it would be worth it to you to have them out of the way and that she could expect a nice little remembrance from you in the mail. You won't forget, will you, sweety?"

"But Grace is a maid. What does she know about taking care of children? Good heaven's, Evelyn, she's the last person I could see tucking them in and reading them a bedtime story. Be more likely to let them run wild while she ran around with that damned husband of hers . . . if he *is* her husband."

"Well, whether he is or not, darling, Grace works for me and she knows if she wants to get paid, she does as I tell her. Let *me* worry about that now, will you? After all, we must keep you calm at all costs, mustn't we?" She looked about her for the first time and missed the slight frown that flickered across Hunter's face, but Ivy did not. From where she had been standing at the back of the hall, uncertain whether or not to come forward to be introduced, she saw both Hunter's look of disappointment and Evelyn's look of disdain and wondered if he were disappointed at his fiancée's lack of warmth. So far, they had not even kissed each other and Ivy had braced herself for that eventuality.

The three of them followed Ivy up the stairs a few minutes later as she showed them to their rooms. She had moved two cots into the large room next to Hunter's and put Bill Walters in her old room, hoping he could survive the rather feminine decor. The bathroom allotment seemed logical and Ivy decided if they were not satisfied, they could shift around to suit themselves. There would probably be some commuting between the two rooms at the front of the house, anyway, she thought with an unexpected thrust. It was unsettling to realize how unwelcome the idea was, for after all, Hunter Smith was nothing to *her* and Evelyn *was* his fiancée.

Dinner was a pot roast, succulent in its brown gravy with a bed of potatoes, carrots, and onions. She had scalloped some of Mattie's home-canned tomatoes and tossed a salad. To follow, there was apple brown Betty, made Mattie's way with black walnuts from their own trees.

Hunter had insisted she join them for dinner, but she refused. It was one thing to share the table with a man who brought his work to his meals and asked nothing of her other than silence. It was quite another to sit across from the beautifully dressed Evelyn and watch her play up to both men.

Ivy had not missed those looks directed at her when Hunter had introduced them and explained that this had once been Ivy's home, though she had been working in town for several years. If looks counted, Evelyn just might be able to accomplish what Ivy herself had not; the termination of her job with Hunter Smith. Conversely, Ivy decided she did not want to leave, regardless of the odd little wrench she felt whenever she saw the two of them together.

A new feeling of restlessness seemed to have come over Hunter; he took to spending more time outdoors and less in the library with his briefcase spilling its contents across the desk. He was not a tidy worker and more than once Ivy had been on the verge of offering her services, but something held her back. It might have been the speculative looks she received from Evelyn Carlin; then again it might have been an instinctive desire to stay away from a man who was proving all too disturbing to her.

Bill Walters sought her out frequently and Ivy found him good company. He seemed interested in her life at Rougemont and she fell into the habit of talking freely with him as she went about her duties. It was hard to resist a friendly overture when it was made over a dishpan, with four hands making light of the work.

It was several days later when she was making the bed in the other woman's room that she overheard a conversation that was not meant for her ears. Bill had taken the jeep to go into Wilksboro and Evelyn and Hunter were in the room below. Ivy had finished the bed and was gathering the strewn garments to rinse out, a chore she resented, when she heard her name drifting up through the open register in the floor.

"She's impossible, Hunt. Where on earth did you find her? Surely she wasn't still hanging around here hoping to be taken on?"

Ivy strained her ears in spite of all the instinct that told her she should leave the room, but she couldn't make out Hunter's reply. Where did he find her, indeed! As if she were something to be picked up on a bargain counter!

"She's utterly unsuitable . . . too young, for one thing . . . nothing like that, of course, for I do know you have better tastes, but . . . bouncing, buxom country type . . . never do!"

The words faded in and out and Ivy simmered. Bouncing, buxom country type, was she? She made her sound like some raw-boned, red-faced nobody! One hundred and four pounds spread over a five-foot-four-inch frame couldn't be all *that* buxom!

She flung out of the room, slamming the door behind her. If they heard her and suspected she had eavesdropped, then well and good. It might teach them to keep their voices down next time they indulged in a spot of vicious gossip.

She met Hunter as she headed for the kitchen, her arms overflowing with Evelyn Carlin's lingerie, and when he would have stopped her, she tossed her head and ignored him, not trusting herself to be civil.

By the end of the week Ivy had made up her mind that Evelyn was not good enough for him. She had learned almost accidentally from Bill Walters that Hunter was far wealthier than she had suspected and far wealthier than Evelyn's first husband, who was almost thirty years her senior. While Bill had not said so, Ivy could tell that he was far from happy at the engagement of the widow to his best friend. Without ever putting it into words, the two of them seemed to share their worry for the man who was growing more and more restless as the days went by.

Not daring to examine her own deepest feelings, Ivy still rebelled at the idea of a marriage between those two. Hunter might not be the easiest man to get along with, as she should know, but he had so much more to offer than Evelyn deserved. She made no bones about being thoroughly bored at Rougemont and did her best to persuade Hunter to close it up and move to Highlands, but he held out against her pleas.

It didn't help matters that the rain continued for days on end, keeping the four of them penned up inside. Hunter closed himself up in the library, despite Bill's objections, and Evelyn flung herself into a chair and leafed nervously through the slick magazines she had brought with her. If she had any interest besides high fashion, Ivy was not to discover it, but then, perhaps if Ivy had looked as stunning in her clothes as the older woman did, she might be more interested, too.

One of Bill's hobbies was woodworking and he was fascinated by the examples he had discovered at Rougemont. In the days when manpower had not been so dear and craftsmanship was prized, someone had taken the time to do some exquisite inlaid paneling at the old house, and even Ivy couldn't remember offhand where other examples of such fine woodworking were to be found.

"Let's go hunting," Bill suggested late one morning when Ivy had finished putting on the ingredients for a pot of rich vegetable soup. "If I promise to help you get lunch on the table, will you give me a guided tour?"

They made only a cursory examination of the ground floor, for Bill had already discovered the gems to be found there, but Ivy took him to see the small room tucked away behind the kitchen.

"There's nothing much here in the way of fancy

work, but I thought you might enjoy the diagonal boarding . . . what you can see over and around the junk, that is."

The room was used as a storeroom for out-of-season linens and discarded furniture and Ivy explained that her grandfather had used it when his arthritis got too bad for the stairs. "He had a shower put in the half bath—no room for a tub—but he hated it. He said if that was all he wanted, he'd take a bar of soap and stand under the downspout."

They climbed the narrow stairs to the unused third floor and as they reached the turn, Hunter called up after them.

"Don't tell me there's a forgotten old Adams mantel up there."

"Join us," Bill urged. "We've run out of the exotic, but the workmanship, Hunt . . . it's superb!"

The third floor was damp and cold, lighted only by a bare bulb that did little to dispel the gloom brought on by the drum of rain on the slate roof and the sullen clouds that seemed to envelop the house itself.

"Watch those beams. They're lethal," Ivy warned, ducking under one of the diagonal braces that ran from the gables.

The Brushy Mountains were obscured by rain, but from another window in the northwest turret, she pointed out the hazy blue line of the Blue Ridge Mountains, visible in the low band of watery sunlight that broke through the heavy gray clouds. She pointed out the features of Grandfather Mountain and felt the warmth radiating from Hunter's body as he moved closer to follow her gaze.

"Cold?" he asked, noticing her sudden trembling.

"N-not really." She grinned, suspecting the tremors were due to more than just the chill in the empty room.

Bill called them over to the the eastern turret to see the yellow, turgid waters of the Yadkin flowing far below, swollen from the days of heavy rain. "Good

thing you don't have to worry about flooding up here
on your red hill," he observed, turning toward the
stairs. "I'm ready for coffee and a warm fire. How
about you two?"

Ivy hesitated only a second before following him, but
that was long enough for Hunter to reach her side and
as if it were the most natural thing in the world, he
dropped a casual arm across her shoulders.

"You *are* cold," he commented, letting his hand run
slowly down her arm to her hand, where his strong
fingers meshed with hers. "Cold hands, warm heart,
isn't that what they say? Is your heart warm, Ivy?"

She couldn't think of a single thing to say in response
to his light banter and she just stood there, kicking
herself for a tongue-tied idiot.

Quickly, he hugged her to his side, as if she were a
niece or a little sister, and told her they'd have to hurry
down to the fire. "We can't have you coming down with
something now," he said, descending the stairs behind
her and closing the door.

They had coffee in the living room with the fire
glowing from the split oak logs Hunter had had
delivered. Evelyn was curled up in one of the wing
chairs looking sulky and neglected and Ivy made an
effort to make conversation with her.

"It looks as if the rain is over for a while. There was a
patch of clear sky over in the west."

"What's the difference! There's nothing to do
here even if the sun shines twenty-four hours a day!
How you ever decided on a place like this, Hunt, I'll
never understand. If you wanted the mountains we
could have found a place at Roaring Gap or Cashiers or
someplace like that. Here you're not even in the real
mountains." She was twisting the magnificent ruby-
and-diamond ring she always wore on her right hand
and Ivy wondered if it were a gift from her late
husband.

It was Bill Walters who answered her. "In case

you've forgotten, Evelyn, Hunt's here for a specific reason and from what I've seen, this place is just what the doctor ordered, in more ways than one."

"With all the conveniences of home, too," Evelyn retorted sarcastically, looking meaningfully at Ivy.

Ivy's eyes flew instinctively to Hunter in time to see a bleak expression flicker across his face, but when Evelyn suggested that the two of them go for a drive, he followed her wordlessly from the room.

They had coffee and sandwiches before the fire, not waiting for Hunter and Evelyn to return, and Bill seemed unusually quiet, almost as if he had something on his mind. The meal was all but over, though, before he asked Ivy if Hunter had mentioned his reasons for coming to Rougemont.

Puzzled, Ivy shook her head. "No, not really. He did say that his company has property all over the country, and I guess he makes the rounds when he can."

"All over the world would come closer to the truth, but that's another matter. You see, to understand why he's here, you have to understand Hunter, himself, and that's not easy."

Ivy agreed all too well, but remained silent, which was just as well, for Bill seemed more intent on whatever was on his own mind than on anything Ivy might offer to the conversation.

"He's a brilliant engineer, but more than that, he's one of the shrewdest business minds I've ever known. Even that, though, might not be enough to get him where he is today if it weren't for the fact that he's been trying to make up for his lack of background all his life. He went through school on scholarships, of course, but after that he was on his own. His parents were dead. . . . Happened when he was about five, I think, and he was brought up by a maternal uncle, a hard-bitten man who taught him that love was something women dreamed up to tie men down with, that money could buy anything, and that you don't trust anyone out of your sight. Nice character, wasn't he? Lord knows what his life was like! Anyway, Hunt drove himself from the time he left school, to make it without having to ask his uncle for a dime and he succeeded beyond anyone's wildest dreams."

The room was silent until the resettling of the glowing logs coincided with a fitful burst of wind against the side of the house. Ivy said it looked as if the clearing was bringing a cold front and Bill continued as if she had not spoken.

"It's that god-awful drive of his that's killing him, Ivy. He was in Kyoto six months ago negotiating with a computer outfit and he started having visual distur-bances. At first he thought it was something he ate, but on a short trip back to the states he got in touch with me and I sent him to N.C. Baptist in Winston-Salem. The upshot of the matter is that if he doesn't let up on about eighty percent of his activities and give his eyes a total rest for three months, he stands a good chance of losing his sight altogether. That's three months in a blindfold, Ivy! Can you imagine the impact of a verdict like that on someone of Hunt's nature?"

Stunned, Ivy could only stare at him. There were so many clues and yet, she would never have imagined such a hellish fate. "But why here?" she managed finally.

"For one thing, the proximity to Baptist Hospital. For another, it's completely off the beaten track, not fashionable or anything like that, thank heavens. He couldn't take being institutionalized for the whole period. Women in white give him the shakes. . . . Might have something to do with the loss of his parents when he was a kid, I don't know. At any rate, the only way he would agree was if he could go someplace alone with someone to keep house and cook and keep him from running into a stone wall until he got the hang of being blind. He's too proud for his own good . . . insists he'll manage as well as a sighted person within a few days and what could I say? It'll be rough enough without my telling him he'll be helpless. As it was, he went back to Kyoto, then on to West Germany before he'd consent to take the cure."

"But where do I come in?" Ivy asked, now thoroughly bewildered. "Surely if anyone should help him through this thing it should be Evelyn . . . Mrs. Carlin.
"

"Did someone take my name in vain, darling?"

Both Ivy and Bill whirled around to see Evelyn shedding her fur coat in the doorway. They had been so intent on what they were discussing they had not even heard the entrance. Ivy looked beyond her, but saw no sign of Hunter.

As if reading her question, Evelyn, whose mood seemed to have undergone a miraculous recovery, exclaimed, "Oh, don't look for Hunt. He's decided to plod along the river or some such nonsense. You may be the first to congratulate me, darlings! I've finally agreed to become engaged to Hunter." With a smile that produced not a single crease in her flawless skin, Evelyn extended her left hand to reveal the ruby-and-diamond ring, now securely settled on the third finger. "What were you saying about me as I came in? Something good, I hope," she quipped brightly, in a manner so totally out of character that Ivy could only stare.

"I've been explaining to Ivy about Hunt's upcoming treatment. She suggested that you would be the logical one to stay with him," Bill informed her in an oddly impassive tone.

"Me! Me? But surely you realize why he needs someone other than me, Ivy. . . . Not that I wouldn't be only too glad to stay with the dear," she hastened to add. "Hunt's a proud animal. He wants someone he cares nothing at all about, someone he can walk away from after the three months are up and never think of again. That's the only way, you see. He couldn't bear for anyone he loved to see him helpless and blind."

With a ringing sound in her ears, Ivy watched as the older woman flung her an openly triumphant look and left the room. She hardly even noticed Bill as he passed a hand wearily over his face and swore softly under his breath.

Chapter Four

It was just after midnight when the phone rang. Ivy had gone up early, hardly expecting to sleep, but as if her strained emotions had triggered an escape mechanism, she fell almost immediately into a deep, dreamless slumber. She blinked awake, dimly aware of the strident summons in the moonlight-silvered room, and at first she didn't stir, knowing Hunter would take it on the extension in his room.

The ringing ceased almost immediately, but to her disgust she found herself unable to get back to sleep. Feeling the beginning of a headache, she gave up and padded down the hall to the bathroom for an aspirin. The cold floor brought her even wider awake. She was thoroughly disgruntled at whoever had aroused the household in the middle of the night, although Hunter received so many overseas calls it was to be expected that occasionally someone would slip up and forget the time difference.

Returning from the bathroom she was just in time to see Evelyn Carlin emerging from Hunter's bedroom. As though someone had struck her a blow in the solar plexus, Ivy froze, and before she could recover and slip away, the older woman glanced up and saw her.

Ivy thought afterward that in the dim light of the hall, she might have imagined the fleeting look of bitter frustration, but there was no mistaking the flash of triumph that followed as Evelyn Carlin flung her a mocking glance and disappeared into her own room.

By the time Ivy came down the next morning, Evelyn was nearly ready to leave. The call, she was told by Bill Walters, who wore a puzzling look of satisfaction, was from the woman who cared for the Carlin children to say that Amy, the oldest, had had an attack of something that looked suspiciously like appendicitis and that Evelyn was needed in case surgery should become necessary.

Bill, who had planned to leave later in the day anyway, drove her to the airport. Before he left, he reconfirmed his plans to meet Hunter at the hospital three days later.

With the morning well under way, Ivy was pushed to get the laundry done before time to prepare lunch. Both guest rooms had to be stripped and remade, and Ivy's mood was not improved by the fact that her headache had returned.

Hunter remained holed up in the library, emerging once, red-eyed and harried, to demand coffee. The phone had rung incessantly and she could hear him all the way back to the kitchen arguing in three languages, occasionally swearing and slamming desk drawers impatiently. He seemed determined to do three months' work in the next three days. Ivy did her best to avoid him, having learned that at times like these, her presence only served to inflame his hair-trigger temper.

Seeing the haggard look on his face when he joined

her for lunch, she recalled Bill's last words as she walked him out to the car while Evelyn was taking leave of her fiancé. He had impressed on her the importance of making Hunter ease up, reminding her that it was stress that had put him in this condition in the first place. As if anything *she* could say would be likely to have any effect.

"You wouldn't want to walk down by the river this afternoon, would you?" she ventured doubtfully, sliding into her chair after putting the salads and casserole on the table.

"Why should I want to walk down by the river?"

"Well, it just might do your disposition some good to get away from that disgusting mess you've made in the library!" she snapped back, illogically hurt that his reaction had been exactly the one she had expected. The library *was* a mess, with maps, charts, and esoteric diagrams of machinery tacked helter-skelter over walls and shelves alike. Every available surface was littered with folders and the illegible notes he scribbled as he talked on the phone. None of which would do him the slightest bit of good, she thought with compunction, when he could no longer see, but he had threatened her life if she so much as moved a pencil.

Hunter was silent so long that Ivy thought she might be back on her way to the unemployment lines again. She sneaked a veiled glance through her lashes and caught a look of speculation on his face.

"You might just have an idea there," he allowed. "In fact, as long as the weather holds, it wouldn't hurt to familiarize myself with the surrounding territory in case I have to blunder out with my head in a sack."

"Oh, Hunter!" Her spoon clattered against the table as it fell from her fingers.

There had not been the slightest trace of self-pity in his voice or on those hard, implacable features; nevertheless, the idea of someone proud to the point of arrogance having to be led about by the hand sent a shaft of pain through her body.

They walked for hours in the quiet, late-November woods. On that first day they followed the riverbank and Ivy showed him the remains of the boat house that had been in use when her father had been a boy and told him about the rafts she had built with Finley when they were both small, causing old Lionel to forbid them the river.

"And that ended your seagoing career?" he asked, a crooked smile lighting his features as if he could visualize a skinny, freckled girl wading out into the muddy waters to launch a ramshackle raft.

"Certainly not. We simply moved our base of operations. There's a place just downstream from here where the river narrows and the water rushes over the rocks. It's full of hidden snags. Granddaddy was always afraid we'd capsize there and knock ourselves silly."

"But you lived to tell the tale."

They were strolling back slowly now, and a carpet of yellow leaves cast up a strange, golden glow in the dusk as she told him of a place just beyond the narrows where the Yadkin widened out and slowed to its usual tranquil pace.

"Even after days of heavy rains, when the rest of the river is hell-bent to reach the Kerr Scott Reservoir and the ocean beyond, it's always quiet in this pool tucked up under the point. That's where we moved our marina; but of course, it was never as exciting after that."

"You didn't value your neck?"

"It never occurred to me that it was in danger," she told him candidly. "At that age, I don't suppose one considers such things as mortality."

Somehow, as if it were the most natural thing in the world, Hunter's hand had found her own and they swung together in a firm, if casual grip.

"It wasn't until I moved to Charlotte," she continued thoughtfully, "that I began to thirst for peace and tranquillity."

"Rougemont?"

"Mmmhmmm. I'm afraid so."

"Why afraid?" When he dropped her hand to allow her to precede him through an opening in a barbed-wire fence, Ivy felt the loss to an unsettling degree.

She shrugged. "It doesn't strike me as wise to become too attached to something that doesn't belong to you," she declared, suddenly painfully aware of the deeper meaning to her words. "Anyway, it's past time I learned to stand alone." She made an effort to sound bright and eager, but was not certain how successful she was when she felt his eyes upon her.

Hunter was more distracted than usual at dinner and immediately afterward he shut himself into the library where he remained until after Ivy had gone to bed.

The next afternoon they walked again. This time they turned northwest to climb the wooded hills that overlooked the fertile bottomlands and Ivy described how they looked in the summertime, all green-gold with corn and tobacco.

"It was all Rougemont land once," she told him with more than a hint of pride, "but gradually Granddaddy sold it off. He couldn't farm it himself and Daddy didn't want to work it. Besides, it costs a heap to maintain a place like Rougemont, as you no doubt will find out." She gave him a mischievous look which went unnoticed as he asked, "Didn't your grandfather mind when his only son wasn't interested in taking up the reins?"

"I guess so. No, I'm sure he minded, not that I ever heard him complain about it. He did say once that he couldn't blame Daddy for the wandering blood in his veins because it was that same blood that carried the first de Coursey from France to this country and a later one up from Baton Rouge to settle here in North Carolina." She swung down and gathered a handful of dried seeds from a tall stem, scattering them to the winds. "He joined the Coast Guard, you know. My daddy, that is. He had always wanted to go to sea, but before he was sent to the North Atlantic he was stationed at Hatteras and he met and married my

mother there. She died when I was born and after
Daddy's hitch in the Coast Guard was up, he went into
the merchant marine."

"Do you see him often?"

She shook her head and pretended a deep interest in
a young bare-topped maple whose remaining leaves
clustered about the base of its branches like a scarlet
tutu.

They reached the old cemetery and she told him
about the first Lionel and his wife, Gillian.

"From the dates, I'd say he wasn't above a bit of
cradle snatching," Hunter observed, brushing the
leaves away from a mossy stone with the tip of his boot.

"He was forty-two and she was seventeen when they
were married, according to the family Bible. There was
some story about his having left Louisana in a hurry,
but I was never certain if it was because of his child
bride or the money he had with him. He evidently had a
bundle, because they built Rougemont within a few
years."

"Child or not, she certainly knew a good thing when
she saw it."

Puzzled, Ivy frowned up at him.

"What woman won't latch on to a meal ticket when
she gets a chance, especially if it promises caviar
instead of corn bread?" He shrugged.

Incensed on behalf of her ancestress, Ivy retorted
angrily, "For your information, Hunter Smith, Gillian
adored her Lionel!"

"And how would you know that? Family Bible tell
you so?" Hunter parried, openly amused at the militant
sparkle in her eyes.

"Money alone won't do a darned thing! It took a lot
of hard work to clear this land and build on it and
Gillian worked right alongside her husband! Besides, if
she had wanted an easy life she would never have
followed him all the way to Wilkes County."

Hunter remained silent and as they gradually turned
homeward, some of Ivy's resentment faded. She re-

called what Bill Walters had said about Hunter's background and she wondered what faint memories lingered on to account for such cynicism. Or had it been acquired at a later date?

They paused before climbing the final hill, the hill for which the house had been named. Sunset bathed an eroded bank of burnt-sienna earth with a crimson glow and poured its warmth over the old brick structure at the crest. Recalling Sam MacNeely's remarks on the night of the party, Ivy smiled to herself; it really *did* resemble a giant pink wedding cake with its turrets and gables all adorned with gingerbread and the ornate lightning rods sparkling like fancy candles.

"Share the joke?" Hunter teased, removing a leaf from her hair. The once-neat chignon had suffered, as it always did, from the walk through the woods.

She told him of Sam's description on the night of the ill-fated party and he laughed, throwing back his head in a gesture far removed from the more usual one of kneading the muscles at the back of his neck. Before she could dwell on his amazingly varied moods, Hunter went on to discuss the house.

"You seldom see that style constructed of brick. I'd be willing to bet they're local bricks, at that."

"I wouldn't know, although there is a brick works further north, I think." She paused to glance up at a squirrel who nibbled at a pinecone and tossed the pieces down at them with a brash impudence. "Lots of people have made fun of it. . . . It is a little pretentious, I suppose, but I've always loved it. Fin did, too . . . still does. Any purity of style is long gone, of course, since Granddaddy added the gables and had the kitchen enlarged. I think he once had some idea about finishing off the third floor, to make room for scads of little de Courseys, but it didn't work out that way. The three of us rattled around in it, and then there were only two of us—and Mattie, of course."

Hunter slipped a companionable arm across her shoulders and together they mounted the hill. Ivy was tremulously aware of the warmth of his hard body, the length of his thigh as it brushed against her own, and she hoped if he noticed the unevenness of her breathing he'd put it down to the exertions of the climb.

They paused outside the back door and Hunter began picking the beggar's-lice, those persistent little seeds, from her jeans and jacket.

"Hold still," he commanded, swatting her playfully on the behind.

"You tickle!"

"If you think *that* tickles," he began, reaching out to pull her against him. One hand began running up and down her side and Ivy wriggled, laughing helplessly.

"Stop!" she cried, trying to twist away but weak with laughter and whatever else it was that dissolved the strength in her lower limbs.

He caught her by the nape and pulled her to him. Off balance, she tumbled into his arms and they tightened about her as their mingled laughter vaporized on the chill air.

It was almost too dark to see his expression for he stood silhouetted against the faded glow of the sky. As he loomed closer, Ivy's eyelids became unaccountably heavy.

His warm, firm mouth closed over her own and something flickered along her nerves, touching off brushfires that threatened to rage out of control as she felt him press her even closer to the growing urgency of his hard body. This was ridiculous, wildly dangerous, her mind kept trying to tell her body, but her body was helplessly delinquent where Hunter was concerned.

Like a dash of ice water on her overheated senses, Finley's voice rang out against the stillness. Ivy flung up her head and felt Hunter stiffen, but he did not release her until after Finley appeared around the corner of the house.

"Where the devil have you been? I've been trying to reach you for hours. I thought maybe you'd decided to chuck it in and go back to Lancing."

At the look Ivy flung at him, he backed away, protesting laughingly, "Only joking, only joking!"

"Did you want something specific or may we look on this as a social call?" Hunter demanded witheringly.

From the corner of her eye, Ivy could see the look of hauteur that was second nature to him and she felt oddly defensive, although on whose behalf, she couldn't say.

"You two have met?" she asked in a small voice.

"Yes, when I took the affairs of this place into my own hands," Hunter confirmed without looking at her. His eyes bored into Finley and the younger man lost a degree of his usual brash assurance.

"As a matter of fact, I wanted Ivy," Finley asserted.

"What do you need, Fin?" she asked him, leading the way into the kitchen to put the kettle on for coffee.

"Sam and Micki are back and Sam brought along a lady and some fellow he wants me to meet. We thought we'd go out to the club for late supper and dancing. Sam, his lady friend, and the four of us—that is, if you'll come."

While Ivy was still searching her mind for an excuse, Hunter took the matter out of her hands.

"Sorry, it's quite impossible," he apologized coolly, and, Ivy was sure, insincerely. "I'm leaving first thing in the morning and there are still several matters to be looked into before I go. I'm afraid I can't spare Miss de Coursey tonight."

Ivy had almost forgotten his appointment at the hospital, so magic a hiatus these past few days had been, and now she wondered anxiously what needed doing to prepare for it. Knowing Hunter, if he said there were things to be done, there were things to be done!

After Hunter had made it unmistakably clear that there would be no time for personal pleasures in the near future, it was not many minutes before Finley put down his coffee cup and stood up to go. He bade them good night, expressing regrets, and Ivy felt her face begin to burn at the speculative looks he cast at Hunter, at her, and back to Hunter again.

With his going went the last of Hunter's mellow mood. Back to the cold war with a vengeance, Ivy thought, plunging a dish into hot suds. Hunter was in the library on the phone again and Ivy judged from the Spanish he employed so fluently that he must be talking to Señor Rivera, who called sometimes twice a day and, depending on how excited he was, spoke less English than the other callers from Miami.

He coped with the man in Stuttgart with equal ease, making Ivy, who barely scraped through high-school French, feel terribly provincial. She had gathered from Bill that he dealt in innovative machinery for recovering oil from hard-to-tap sources. . . . That was the German firm, and the Spanish must have to do with a plant in Puerto Rico, headquartered in Miami, that manufactured medically oriented electronic components. How many other enterprises came under the shawl of HS Engineering, Incorporated, she had no idea. Bill, himself, headed the Atlanta branch of the industrial health-care program Hunter had recently set up for his employees.

At half past ten Ivy decided to go to bed. Hunter showed no signs of flagging and if his personal empire couldn't do without his constant supervision, then there was nothing Ivy could do about it at this late date.

As she reached the stairs, he emerged, hair on end and chamois shirt opened all the way to his low-slung belt, to demand where she was going.

"To bed," she told him flatly, resenting his peremptory tone of voice even as she saw with compunction the gray weariness that had shaded his features.

"Sorry I got tied up, but there's still the room to be done."

"What room?" She moved slowly back down the steps. As he towered over her she regretted having taken off her wedgies.

"I want the room next to the kitchen cleared out while I'm gone and I thought we'd make a start tonight. If you'll empty the wardrobe, I'll bring down the things from my closet, then you can do the rest while I'm away. I don't intend to be an invalid, but there's no point in tempting fate by tackling those stairs. The room down here will be perfectly adequate, as it has its own bath, so let's get it converted, shall we?"

"Now?" She could not hide her dismay, for it had been a long day and she was more than ready to retire.

"Yes, now!" He ran a hand across the back of his neck in the familiar gesture. Then Ivy was given a crooked smile that lighted his eyes like the sun on stormy waters.

"Sorry, girl," he apologized tiredly. "I've got a merger coming to a head, a seven-figure bid due in two weeks, and as if that weren't enough, an elusive little microelectronics genius I've been courting for a year finally shows signs of taking my bait. Of all times to be sidelined . . . !"

"You haven't had your nightly whiskey, have you?" Ivy offered impulsively. He badly needed something to relax the tension that creased his brow and brought that clamped-down look to his wide, sensuous mouth.

"No, but I have something else in mind for tonight, as a matter of fact. I had planned on a celebration send-off dinner and I stashed away a bottle of good champagne. The dinner didn't work out, but there's no reason we can't open the bottle of wine."

She gave in immediately, in spite of a small warning voice that told her she was courting danger. "Fine, but first I'll clear out the wardrobe. Then, if you'll give me five minutes, I'd love a shower. What with one thing and another, I hardly had time to even wash my face before dinner and I can't drink champagne in tatty jeans."

"You've got it. There's still time for a respectable toast or two before you turn into a pumpkin. Let me tape a few more notes for my assistant in Altanta before I haul down the contents of my closet and join you in the living room."

The wardrobe contained only a pair of dry-rotted draperies and an ancient raincoat of Mattie's that she had used for feeding the chickens in the days when Rougemont kept its own hens. Ivy was through and upstairs before Hunter finished taping his notes. Shucking out of her jeans, she plunged under a hot shower.

After drying herself and slathering on a scented lotion, she decided on a velvet caftan in an eastern print of gold and rust on gray that had cost far too much, even on sale, last fall. There had been few occasions to wear it, but it was far and away the most glamorous thing she had ever owned. The thought hovered in the back of her mind that this was the picture of her he would carry with him—supposing he *did* carry one—and she pushed aside the prodding of her conscience that whispered that she was dressing up for a man who was engaged to someone else.

Just for tonight, she breathed softly, leaning toward the mirror to apply a smooth film of lip gloss, and then I'll become the model housekeeper I was hired to be, one who can be left at the end of three months with no regrets on either side.

Hunter was downstairs before her, his hair crinkling wetly around the edges from the shower and his lean body splendidly set off by dark-green suede pants and a matching knit shirt that laced halfway down the front, revealing the thatch of dark hair on his chest. He bore little resemblance to the conservative, cold businessman who had turned up on the front porch not long ago—except for the air of authority he had worn like a royal robe, but then, Ivy suspected, that had more to do with the man than the clothes.

"Settle down . . . over there." He nodded to the sofa before he thumbed the cork. "I put on another of the apple logs, smell it?"

She inhaled the subtle fragrance and tucked her

feet up under her and moments later, raising a stem to hers, Hunter offered a toast. "To good fortune; may she reward the deserving and be tolerant of the unworthy."

They sipped the wine and Ivy felt a strange compulsion as she gazed across the effervescing glass into Hunter's eyes. The expression in them was disconcerting. She broke out nervously, "And are you among the former or the latter?"

"The latter, to be sure, but I hope both you and Lady Luck will be tolerant." A smile simmered slowly beneath the cool surface of his eyes, weakening the pitiful defenses Ivy tried to erect against his experienced charm; she glanced at him again through the veil of her dark lashes. In her overstimulated imagination, his eyes were playing dangerous games with her—at least she'd be safer in thinking it was her own imagination. It would be fatal to take him seriously, for he was not hers to be taken, seriously or otherwise.

"This is more potent than I remembered," she said breathlessly as he topped off her glass. "The last time I had champagne was . . . let's see, when Fin passed his exams and became a licensed real-estate broker. I don't think it was as good as this, though," she judged. "Or maybe it was only because it was my first."

"I suspect you and Hooper share a good many firsts," Hunter remarked obliquely. "He's a handsome enough devil."

"Yes, he is, isn't he? I always used to think he was beautiful and he got furious with me when I told him so. He said it was handsome in a man, beautiful only in a woman, which is silly, I think." She was dimly aware that she was beginning to babble and made an effort to restrain herself. She was not an experienced enough drinker to know the full effects of alcohol on her system but she wanted to avoid the embarrassment of becoming maudlin.

The air between them suddenly seemed to drop several degrees in temperature and Hunter leaned back to study her almost insolently. "I'm afraid you'll have to curb your enthusiasm as far as your sweetheart is concerned," he said with a return of the familiar bleak coolness.

"What do you mean?"

"Just that for the next three months you'll be completely responsible for the house as well as my own welfare and you'll have no time for lover boy," he pointed out disparagingly. "I'm paying you five thousand dollars; enough, I believe, to entitle me to your full attention, and that means I don't want your lover hanging around here to distract you, is that clear?"

"Stop calling him that! He . . . he's . . ." Her voice broke under his cold sarcasm and she took a deep breath and added, "Besides, I told you, I don't want your old money!"

"No, of course you don't," he jeered. "You're staying on out of pure goodness, a real little humanitarian, aren't you?"

"D-darn you, I t-told you . . ." she was chattering furiously, hating herself for being shattered so easily by this infuriating man. He controlled her emotions as if he were a puppeteer and she dangled helplessly from his strings!

"Nothing could make me stay now!" she vowed, blinking away the treacherous wetness in her eyes. She jumped to her feet, swaying dangerously, and before she could recover, he had grabbed her wrist and toppled her back onto the sofa.

"Sit down!" he barked after the fact. "You'll find a verbal contract quite binding in case you had any ideas about running out on me. If the thought of doing without your boyfriend tears you up like this," he sneered, "I'll try to arrange an occasional meeting, but on my terms, understand?"

"And just what terms are those?" she demanded weakly, unable to pull her wrist away from his brutal grasp.

His eyes roved restlessly over her face, making her suddenly conscious that tears had probably washed away the light dusting of powder she had used to cover her freckles.

"I'll let you know," he told her gruffly.

The fire settled noisily, showering sparks against the screen as the two people stared relentlessly at each other, locked in a silent combat of wills. Ivy made heroic efforts to control the wobble of her chin, determined not to allow him to see how easily he could wound her. Darn the champagne, she thought belligerently. It had weakened her resistance disastrously!

She was completely unaware that the tears were still overflowing her sea-gray eyes until Hunter raised a brown hand, extended one finger and carefully wiped a cheek. Numbly, she noted the darkening of his eyes to a shade just short of black.

There was a certain inevitability about the slow movement that pulled her across the intervening space until she rested against the rock-hard muscles of his chest. His hands played sensuously across her back through the velvet and she knew he was well aware that there was nothing to impede his explorations.

He was in no hurry. Ivy was utterly helpless against him, as if her bones had turned to warm wine, her blood to drugged honey. Only when his hands moved to cup her breast, his thumbs sending messages through her body as they moved slowly back and forth across the exquisitely sensitive tips, did some vestige of self-preservation make her draw away.

"Hunter, please," she whispered, struggling in slow motion to escape the powerful compulsion of his touch. She knew her own vulnerability under the best of circumstances; she was utterly helpless to resist this enigmatic man who, in spite of all the angry words they traded, had only to touch her. And now, after two glasses of champagne . . . !

"Please," she whispered again, fighting against the

fatal languor that had stealthily invaded her lower limbs.

"You don't have to beg, Ivy," he replied in a low rumble that vibrated along her spine. Was there a hint of amusement in his voice?

There was! She pulled away, glaring at him suspiciously, and he allowed her to gain her feet, unsteady though they were. When he made no effort to restrain her, she was illogically piqued, but she told him with all the dignity she could muster that she was going to bed.

"Is that an invitation?"

"No, it is not!" she denied hotly, only to be thrown into utter confusion by the laughter that spilled from him. He was treating the whole thing as a joke!

"I'm going to the hospital first thing in the morning. Will you kiss me good-bye?" he asked softly, twin devils dancing in his eyes.

"Are you trying to play on my sympathies?" she demanded suspiciously.

"Would it do any good?"

She hesitated, then cautiously leaned down to brace her hands against his shoulders as she touched his lips with hers.

He did not move, his lips warm, firm, and completely still beneath her own, and yet, as she reluctantly raised her head, she had the oddest sensation that he was drawing her back to him.

She stood there, staring down at him in bewilderment, and as if her own hesitancy triggered his response, he struck with lightninglike rapidity and she was once more tumbled, this time across his lap.

Expertly, he turned her and bore her back against the cushions, parting her lips demandingly. She struggled, some remnant of sanity warning her against the treachery of her own defenses as the fever of his thudding urgency transmitted itself to her own body.

"Ivy, oh, Ivy . . . how I want you," he breathed against the wild pulse at the base of her throat.

Her caftan had slipped from her shoulders, its intricate design lending itself ingeniously to Hunter's searching hands, and now he was tasting the silky flesh of her breasts.

Ivy was beyond caring, lost to the point where she wanted only to give in to his demands, to reap the promised ecstasy. Her hands were moving over his back, and as they moved around his waist they touched the cold metal buckle of his belt.

Her fingers froze. Nothing in her past had even faintly prepared her for the tumultuous demands of her own passion and now it was instinct alone that firmed her resolves. One minute . . . sixty seconds more, and she would have been irredeemably lost. This she knew with a devastating certainty, for even as her brain was clamoring that he did not love her, could never be a part of her life, her shuddering body was crying out for release from this overwhelming burden of desire.

"Ivy, Ivy, don't stop now . . . please, darling!" he groaned, as she pulled away from him.

"Oh, Hunter, it's crazy! It's impossible!" She could have wept for the agony in her heart as he stiffened and drew himself up to sit hunched over the edge of the sofa.

"Oh, Ivy," he exclaimed softly, running an unsteady hand through his hair down to the back of his neck.

Silently pleading for understanding and support, Ivy reached out to touch his shoulder, but he jumped up as if her touch were a burning brand. Her eyes followed him as he came to a halt on the other side of the room, facing out into the darkness as if his only hope of salvation lay in the stars that blinked mockingly through the bare branches outside.

Hopelessly, she stared at the gleaming boots, braced against the old faded Rabat rug, at the well-shaped calves and powerful thighs so aggressively delineated in the suede pants, past narrow hips and loin to the threatening breadth of his shoulders. He looked coiled, ready to strike, and irrelevantly, Ivy recalled Bill's words about the ferocious games of racketball he engaged in after a day at the conference table.

Now he was using her to work off his frustrations and hostilities. Before she could accuse him of it, though, he turned on her, his eyes burning with an intensity that took her breath away.

"Girl, you play a pretty rough game."

So startled was she at his uncanny ability to tune in on her wavelength, she could only stare at him. Then, gathering up her tattered defenses, she told him, "As . . . as a substitute player, I . . . I wasn't quite sure of the rules."

"Substitute?"

She would not have attributed acting to his plentiful talents, but he was obviously a past master.

"Evelyn," she reminded him. "You must be missing her dreadfully to . . . to put up with such a p-poor substitute."

"Ah, yes . . . my esteemed fiancée," he remarked silkily, fast regaining his poise, if, indeed, he had ever lost it. "But then, since I interrupted your own plans for an evening out with your blond Adonis, I felt compelled to make up for it."

She cringed, suddenly miserably aware of the spectacle she must make, still sprawled on the sofa, her hair tumbled across her back and her caftan sloping down one shoulder. Embarrassment made her flare out at him. "Well, I'm sorry, but I don't care for substitutes, myself! Nor do I think poor Evelyn would appreciate your lapse. Maybe you'd better marry her and be done with it, since waiting doesn't seem to suit you very well!"

"Maybe you're right! After all, if I were married, then I could dispense with your services," he sneered. "Look at all the money I'd save."

"Knowing Evelyn, I somehow doubt that." Despite being under his eagle eyes, she couldn't resist making furtive efforts as she spoke to straighten out her clothing.

"As far as that goes, I'd say you were about as desperate for a man as I am a woman, so you might consider putting Hooper out of his misery. Happy endings all around, right?"

"I think I'd better go," Ivy muttered, seeing no way to settle the situation with any degree of grace. Before she had even gained the hall, she heard the clink of bottle against glass. She wished she could drink herself into some sort of oblivion.

There'd be no forgetting this night; that she knew with a painful resignation. With her hand on the knob of her door, she hesitated, eyes watering disgracefully again, and considered turning the key in the lock. Then she moved away. There'd be no need for such a gesture, of that she was somehow certain; she couldn't tell if her choked sobs were from humiliation or disappointment.

She did not see Hunter again until two days later, when he arrived with Bill Walters. Bill got out of the car first and Ivy, who had run outdoors at the first sound of the Jensen's distinctive purr, was on hand to greet him. Enveloped in a friendly bear hug, she didn't see her employer until he stood beside her, dressed once more in a sober business suit, his black tie matching exactly the narrow band of silk across his eyes.

The shock brought an involuntary gasp. She didn't know quite what she had expected; bandages, perhaps, or a hood of some sort, but there was nothing at all to indicate the invalid, unless it was a trace more pallor than was usual.

"Hunter?" she spoke tentatively. She had made a strong effort to forget what had happened the night before he left, telling herself it was the normal result of an undeniable physical attraction and too much champagne, but it all came flooding back at the sight of him.

"Give me your hand, Ivy," he ordered peremptorily. She did as he asked and felt a current flowing between them that left her shaken. If he felt anything at all, he gave no indication, but then, no doubt years of experience had left him well insulated.

"You may lead me to the bottom of the steps and that's the beginning and the end of your duties as a lead dog," he announced with all his old arrogance. He tugged her forward impatiently, betraying a certain nervousness only by the faintest line of white around his nostrils.

Before she could recover her equilibrium, they were at the base of the seven steps that led up to the wide front porch and at her hesitation, Hunter dropped her hand and proceeded to climb the stairs with a deliberation that bespoke intense concentration. She stood in awe as he crossed the porch with barely a trace of hesitation and extended his hand only a few inches from the door latch, correcting almost immediately.

Without a word to the two people who stood watching from the driveway below, he opened the door and disappeared inside.

"Well, I'll be," Bill exploded softly. "The proud devil said he'd do it, but I didn't believe him."

"Can he see at all?"

"Not on your life. Don't let that suave Manhattan look fool you; under the black-silk surface is an extremely efficient pad that removes all temptation to peep without exerting any pressure on the eyes, themselves. He's under strictest orders not to remove it except for sleeping and showering in a dark room, and, Ivy, it's up to you to see that he follows those orders to the letter. If he gets obstreperous, you'll just have to lock him in the bathroom and unscrew the light bulb."

Uncertain of whether or not he was joking, Ivy gave him a sidewise glance. She was none the wiser by the time Bill hefted the two overnighters and his black medical bag and shooed her forward.

"Come on, honey, he'll be in there on the phone if

we don't stop him. That's another thing. . . . Work hours are curtailed to no more than three a day. If he shows signs of getting too upset, give him one of the capsules I'll leave with you."

"Curtailed by whom?" Ivy asked doubtfully, more than a little bewildered by the rapid changes her preconceived ideas were undergoing. Instead of a nursemaid to cut his food and lead him around, it sounded as if she were to play the part of warden.

"Curtailed by you, little lady. That's what you're here for, remember?" Bill replied, confirming her suspicions. "He has some of the most capable men in the industry working for him; in fact, he wouldn't have any other kind, but he won't give them any scope at all. I don't mind telling you, the Atlanta crowd is glad he's going to be out of commission for a while. He can be difficult to work for, but fair, too honest for his own good."

"Don't I know it!" she breathed softly, following Bill's lanky form through the hallway to put Hunter's bag in his room. He was there, carefully feeling his way around from straight chair to double bed to ungainly wardrobe and back again. Ivy wondered how he managed to move so surely in an unfamiliar room; anyone else would have knocked over something by now.

Of course, he did have an extraordinary amount of will, as well as a high degree of sensitivity. In *some* areas, that was. She recalled what Evelyn had said about his not wanting anyone he cared about to see him helpless: he need not have worried. There was nothing even faintly helpless about the man who could function so efficiently with the sudden loss of one of his senses.

Bill stayed two days during which he instructed Ivy against any eventuality, giving her medicine for the possible severe headaches that could occur as well as the tranquilizers he had promised. When he assured her of his complete faith in her ability to cope with the case, Ivy considered his attitude kind, but overoptimistic. However, he also told her to get in touch with him about anything that came up, that he could be at Rougemont within a matter of hours.

"I'm not really all that necessary in Atlanta in spite of Hunt's efforts to make me feel indispensable. He may or may not have told you, Ivy, but he rescued me after I hit bottom. Family problems . . . drinking . . . bad scene. Anyway, I love him like a brother, but I'm not blind to his faults. Don't baby him, and don't let him run all over you," he advised her. "He's a tyrant at the best of times and he's bound to be in a foul humor, at least at first."

The words were prophetic. As Hunter grew more and more morose and irritable Ivy was often reduced to tears by nightfall. He railed against her, using every verbal weapon at his disposal and the arsenal was comprehensive. When she could take no more, she escaped to the shed where she pounded away at a slab of silver she had laboriously sawed out ages ago with some idea of forming a brooch.

It had been so long since the chimney had been inspected that she was afraid to light the wood-burning stove, but her temper kept her warm enough as she sawed and soldered, hammered and annealed. Heaven only knew what the thing would look like when it was finished, for design had never been her strong point. She had taken a course at Arts and Crafts Association while she was in school in Winston-Salem, though, and as she still had both tools and materials, she kept at it sporadically, for lack of something else to do.

At the end of the first week, Evelyn phoned. Ivy answered the call in the library as Hunter was still in his room, and before she could summon him, Evelyn took the opportunity to ask about Ivy's future plans.

"While we're honeymooning, I suppose you'll be looking for another job, won't you? Hunter will sell Rougemont as soon as the three months is up, I suppose, because he knows I can't stand the place and besides, he won't want to be reminded of anything connected with it once we leave. When I talked to him the other night he said he was bored stiff."

"Under the circumstances, that might not be a bad thing," Ivy retorted sharply. "Bill says he needs to let up on work and get as much rest as possible. I'm sure his future health is worth a few weeks of boredom." Not that she could imagine his ever being bored. He had too good a mind for that.

"Bill's an old maid. Hunt will never be satisfied to lie around doing nothing. . . . That is unless he has someone with him to make lying around a pleasure. Wouldn't you just love to take on that little chore, though?"

At Ivy's indignant gasp, the other woman continued, "Oh, don't think we haven't had some laughs over your silly little infatuation, but Hunt's not one to let it bother him. He's had women hanging out after him since his prep-school days . . . before that, probably. He might even make a pass at you if things get dull enough around there, but don't think it means anything, sweety, because once he's served his time, he'll be gone from there so fast you won't even see his dust, and then guess who will be waiting to become Mrs. Hunter Evanston Smith the third?"

"If you're all that anxious to marry him, why wait?" Fortunately, anger disguised the humiliation Ivy felt.

"Oh, come on now, even a little country queen like you can figure that one out. A millionaire under forty is something to capture, but a *blind* millionaire under forty is something else again. Let's just say I know my limitation and playing nursemaid to an invalid for the next half a century isn't my idea of good, clean fun. Although I'll grant you, Hunter is almost worth it. As you no doubt have discovered for yourself, his talents aren't strictly limited to making money."

The meaning in her voice was unmistakable and it was several seconds before Ivy could speak. She had held no great opinion of Evelyn Carlin in the first place, but to hear the brutal truth spoken in such an unabashed manner left her stunned and aching for the man who planned to spend the rest of his life with such a woman. Not that marriage was such a life sentence these days; still, she knew instinctively that to Hunter, it would be no less than a lifetime commitment.

As for Evelyn's other statement, that they had laughed together at Ivy's silly infatuation, well, she could not believe it. For the sake of her sanity and her pride, she could not allow herself to believe that, because if she did, she would have to go.

"If you'll wait a minute, I'll put Hunter on," she managed finally, putting the receiver down with a crash that threatened the ivory plastic . . . and an ivory ear on the other end, she sincerely hoped!

After he took the call in the library behind closed doors, Ivy heard Hunter wander into the living room where he switched on the radio and twirled the dial restlessly. She was constantly amazed at the uncanny ease with which he got around, even considering that he had so far limited his territory to the front part of the first floor. He would not allow Ivy to do anything for him unless it was absolutely necessary. For the most part, she found it wisest to remain just out of range, watchful in case he should need her, but not intruding on his obsessive need to be independent.

Still shaken from her conversation with his fiancée, she decided to have an early night rather than share the intimacy of music and firelight with him in the living room. She could not trust herself not to explode should Evelyn's name be mentioned. Besides, watching him—the odd combination of arrogance and vulnerability, his rakish charm only emphasized by the narrow black band that hid his eyes—sometimes it was all she could do not to touch him. There was a sort of refined torture in being so close, so free to feed her growing attraction with the sight of him, knowing it would all end within a matter of weeks.

There was no longer any doubt in her mind about her own motivation for staying. Rougemont was secondary, nor did she particularly mind if she never saw Finley again. She just might have to use him as a red herring, however, to disguise her growing love for Hunter, should the occasion arise. She considered he owed her that for getting her involved in this impossible situation in the first place.

"I'm going up," she declared to the handsome figure brooding, whiskey in hand, in the largest wing chair. "Can I get you anything before I go?"

"Excitement too much for you, I guess," he jeered. "What do you do up there every night, read? Or talk on the phone to your lover? You can't sleep fourteen hours every night."

Patience, she cautioned herself . . . loving is not always liking. "I read until I get sleepy. Why? Does it really matter to you what I do?"

"Not a bit. As long as you keep the house ticking over and serve meals on time, you can do what you very well please!"

Stung into indiscretion, she flung at him, "Well, in that case, maybe I'll drive into Wilkesboro and see my lover in person. It's so much more satisfactory, don't you think?"

"You're not to leave this house without my permission! Now, get out! Go to bed! What are you hanging around here for, my heartfelt thanks for your tender loving care?" Then, as if tiring of his nightly game of baiting her, he said tiredly, "Go to bed, Ivy. I can't stomach the thought of you moping around here with a wounded look on your tearful little face."

Strangling back a retort, Ivy marched from the room. How could she ever have thought she loved a man who could treat her so brutally? There were times when she wanted to throw herself at him and tear her nails down his face . . . and then there were times when she wanted to throw herself at him so he could trigger all that special magic for her again.

She must have slept several hours when the phone awakened her. The thought of Hunter's stumbling around downstairs trying to answer it made her hurry down the hall to the upstairs extension before she realized how stupid she was being; Hunter was far more at home in the dark than she would ever be.

"Ivy? Is that you?" came the disembodied voice at the other end.

"Finley! What do you want this time of night?" she demanded angrily, her voice lowered against the possibility of waking Hunter. After tonight's clash of tempers, it would be just ducky for him to catch her in a midnight conversation with her so-called lover boy!

"Sorry, Ive, but I'm in a bind."

"I was fast asleep, for heaven's sake!"

"I said I was sorry. Look, Ive, do you know the old Trant place?"

"You woke me up to . . . !"

"Shut up and listen, please, sweetheart, will you?" His strained patience was evident even over the phone. "I'm stuck out here miles from anywhere and there's not a darned thing open at this time of night."

"Then where are you calling from?"

"From a phone booth, stupid. No, wait, don't hang up. Look, do you remember that station at the corner of highway sixteen and Old Sawmill Road? I'm there, where we bought the apples last year. The car's up the road about a mile and a half where you turn off to get to old Trant's permanent pasture."

"What on earth are you doing there?" she sighed, resigned to having to go to the rescue.

"Well, Micki and I kind of moseyed along the Blue Ridge Parkway this afternoon and then we had dinner at Shatley Springs and we were coming home down sixteen when . . ."

"I know . . . when the moon started to rise over Trant's permanent pasture. Lo and behold, you discovered you were out of gas."

"Wrong. Plenty of gas. The car just wouldn't start.

We were only there for half an hour or so, but the thing just wouldn't turn over."

"Wait there," she bade him. "I'll be along as soon as I can."

A feeling of guilt followed her as she shut the back door quietly after her and found her way out to the jeep with the help of a weak flashlight. She had grabbed up her heavy coat to cover her pajamas and rammed her feet into fur-lined boots, but the night air bit sharply into her lungs.

The jeep made its usual uninhibited roar as she eased it away from the shed. She only hoped Hunter had slept through it. If her luck held, she could pick up and deliver Fin and Micki and get back here without his ever knowing she had gone.

Her luck did not hold. An hour and a half later, after dropping off a chagrined Finley and a subdued Micki to their respective apartments, she parked the jeep and crept stealthily up to the back door, which she had left unlatched. Her hand was on the knob when the door was jerked open, tumbling her against the figure that blocked her way.

"Where have you been?" he demanded harshly. "As if I didn't know! He calls and you go running, just like that! It must be terrific to command such devotion!"

"You don't . . ." she began frantically, to be cut off by a sharp pain in her shoulder as he pulled her forcefully through the door and slammed it behind her.

"I don't understand what it's like, is that what you were trying to say? I don't understand what it's like for you not to be able to see your lover whenever the mood strikes you? How do you think I feel with my . . . lover," he spat out the word, "several hundred miles away? Am I supposed to put on the robes of celibacy along with my blindfold?"

He grabbed her arm as she would have escaped him and hauled her roughly against him, grinding his mouth down on hers with a ferocity that was all but out of control. "Was that what you went out for?" he sneered. "You might try the homegrown variety, you could come to appreciate it." He held her so tightly that she was growing dizzy from lack of air. It was as if he wanted to punish her for all the frustrations of being blind, of being apart from Evelyn. . . .

"Please let me go, Hunter," she begged, feeling his hands on the belt of her coat. It slipped from her shoulders and fell to the floor and his marauding mouth moved along the tendon in her neck with a series of nibbling kisses that buckled her knees with weakness. One arm held her against his aroused body while his other hand was moving up under her loose pajama coat, cupping a throbbing breast. He whispered her name over and over against her lips and she hung there helplessly in his arms, too drained to try to escape, even had she wanted to. The hand left her breast, moved to her waistband and circled her navel and she panicked.

"No, Hunter, please . . . no!" Tears were sliding unheeded down her face and she tasted the salt on her lips a moment before his hand came out and touched her cheek in a featherlike gesture.

"Ivy? You're crying," he whispered. "I always make you cry and I never mean to." He touched a tear with the tip of his tongue, his hands now infinitely gentle on her face, and she put up her hands to push him away.

"This is getting to be a habit," he said softly in his deep, gravelly voice. "I can only promise to try . . . that's all. Go to bed now, Ivy, before I take back even that promise."

She turned away, her breath catching on a hard, hurting lump in her throat, and made her way upstairs to fall across her bed, emotionally bankrupt.

Chapter Five

During the days that followed, every instinct for self-preservation screamed at her to go before it was too late, but Ivy knew she was powerless in the face of Hunter's need. As if he sensed her indecision, he maintained an impersonal attitude that was utterly baffling, especially in light of the raw emotions that had precipitated so many conflicts between them.

Ivy went along with it; what else could she do? There was no point in telling herself she was free to leave, for even had Hunter not been so dependent on her, she knew she would stay as long as she possibly could. Right up to the wedding march? she asked herself in a rare burst of masochism.

He worked too hard. Ivy had done her best to suggest that he follow Bill's orders, had even considered calling in Bill to reinforce her, but it would do no real good. Even when he was not working, Hunter was restless, driven to pace and prowl as if he were faced with some insurmountable problem. That his nights were as troubled as his days was evidenced by the rumpled condition of his bed when Ivy went in to do his room each morning after breakfast.

She dared not move a single item of furniture, for once Hunter made his way around a room, touching every chair, every table and lamp, he never fumbled. It was as if he had a photographic memory, and considering the pages of technical data he seemed to devour, perhaps he did. She had heard him on the phone spieling off facts and figures as if he were reading them from a chart in his head.

The man was an enigma. Ivy spent hours in her room with an unread book open in her hands thinking of the many facets of his complex personality. According to Bill, he was a near genius in his field, but when that small, specialized area had begun to expand, he had shown himself to have a first-class business head as well. He could be near omniscient when it came to buying in advance properties that would be needed by his business interests in a few years' time, and on the personal side, he could be, for all his diamond hardness, so achingly tender that Ivy was completely disarmed.

He was also blind, in more ways than one, she reminded herself, recalling his description of Evelyn Carlin as a widow with two small children who needed someone to take care of her.

Evelyn was a widow who needed care like a black-widow spider was a widow who needed care, Ivy thought with an uncharacteristically bitter smile. She was hanging the last of the laundry on the line in the cold December sunshine, and she might wish Hunter's care and sympathy would extend to buying a dryer for her. At the moment, her hands looked like the before part of a lotion advertisement.

Hurrying to the back door with the empty basket, she paused at an unfamiliar sound. It was a whine. She looked over the backyard, grown too high with weeds, and the untended garden, all browned by the killing frosts, and at the corner of the shed she saw a dog.

"Here, boy. Come on, I won't hurt you," she called softly, kneeling and extending a hand.

It took almost five minutes for the pathetic creature to cover the distance, slinking belly down, tail between his legs, and retreating three steps for every four he took, but at last he ventured a cold, wet nose to sniff Ivy's hand.

"There, boy, it's all right, it's all right," she soothed. For all his ribs were not showing, he acted as if he hadn't had a meal in days and was shaking from the cold.

What to do with him presented something of a problem. There had been more than a few bitter jests on Hunter's part about seeing-eye dogs so she didn't have the nerve to turn up with a mutt of any sort, especially one so utterly unprepossessing. Besides, it would never do to have any animal around that might trip him up and she had an idea this creature was not particularly obedient.

Still, she couldn't simply ignore him.

"Come on, sugar, you can go as far as the kitchen. The boss man never goes in there . . . at least not often," she amended ruefully, remembering a night a week earlier.

Rinny—she gave him the secondhand name—had a thorough brushing, which he did not care for; a plate of leftovers, which he practically inhaled; and then he found the warmest spot in the room and circled half a dozen times before dropping. From then on, every move Ivy made was greeted with a pitifully grateful gaze and a thump of his tail.

"You'll have to be my secret, Rinny, love, but it's nice to have a friendly, uncritical face around the house."

She fell into the habit of talking to the hound— softly, to be sure, for she didn't care to have to explain his presence to Hunter. He would probably insist on

papers with any animal he accepted and if poor old
Rinny ever had a pedigree, it was not evident from his
nondescript gray-brown coat, his limp ears, and ingratiating tail.

Evelyn called every other night and as far as Ivy
knew, Hunter called her on alternate nights. He did not
offer any information; indeed, he found little to say to
her these days, other than the occasional comment on
the food she served. He seemed distracted and Ivy
noticed his three-hour work periods were extending to
more like five.

She was amazed when he suggested a walk one
Sunday morning at breakfast.

"I've begun to go stale," he told her, drumming on
the table with nervous fingers. "It suddenly struck me
that I've been shut up inside now far too long. I think I
can make it to the bottom of the hill without falling flat
on my face if you don't mind a spot of guide duty."

If she didn't mind! It had been ages since she had
even touched him and the urge was frighteningly
powerful when she saw him like this, pale and with-
drawn, his hair showing more gray than ever. It was a
good thing he couldn't see her face now, for she could
feel her love shining out like a beacon!

She let her eyes stray over him as he sat there, tensed
and hard in the soft corduroys and knit shirt. He was so
different in some ways from the austere businessman
she had first met, stiff and correct in gray worsted, with
a neat waistcoat delineating his flat torso. Even then,
though, his tough good looks had attracted her far
more than was good for her peace of mind.

Forcing her eyes away from that strong, virile body,
she made herself speak brightly. "We could take a
lunch if you'd like. I used to picnic down by the old
boat house."

"Whatever you say," he agreed evenly.

Poor Rinny had to be left behind with a bone to keep
him entertained. Ivy could not risk his getting underfoot. If today's expedition proved a success, it might

well lead to others and Ivy knew it would be good for Hunter to get outdoors more, for he wasn't sleeping well at all. She could hear him pacing long after she went upstairs, the sounds echoing clearly through the empty rooms.

Of course, she wasn't sleeping well, either, but it was not from a lack of exercise.

He held her arm lightly and she quickly adapted to his longer stride. She tried to maintain her practicality, but it was sheer heaven to feel that firm, warm grip, to brush his hip and thigh as they walked side by side along the narrow path. She was silent, not wanting to break the tentative feeling of camaraderie that seemed to have sprung up between them, and when they reached the site of the boat house without mishap, she led him to where a leaning wall made a natural backrest. He sat there in the sunshine while Ivy unpacked the sandwiches, two apples, and a thermos of coffee.

Protected as he was from the wind by a stand of pines, the sun felt good and Hunter dozed after lunch. Ivy sat cross-legged and watched him, afraid to move even after her legs went to sleep, for fear of disturbing him.

When her cramped limbs protested too much, she eased herself to a kneeling position, still watching Hunter's face. The low angle of the sun revealed new lines in his forehead above the band and there was a shadow of beard on his chin. Thank heaven for electric razors, she thought with a wry grin. At least she didn't have to worry about that!

She put one booted foot on the ground in order to rise, causing the dry leaves to rustle beneath her.

"Where are you going?" Hunter asked.

"I thought you were asleep."

"I am." He grinned, deepening the creases in his lean cheeks.

"Ah ha! A sleep talker!"

"A man can't be held responsible for what he says

under those conditions." He pulled his knees up before him, stretching the jeans tightly over his powerfully muscled thighs.

"I promise I won't hold you responsible for any state secrets you give away between snores," Ivy teased, tucking the thermos back into the canvas bag she had brought.

There was a pause and she looked at the sun, considering reluctantly that it was time to start back.

"Would you hold me . . . period?" he asked, without turning his face toward her. There was a strange note in his voice, almost an uncertainty.

"What do you mean?" she asked breathlessly, drawing closer in spite of herself.

"Just that. Would you hold me?"

"Yes . . . I think I would."

"Well?" he prompted after several moments of silence.

As if in a dream, Ivy knelt down beside him. His hands reached up, bumping awkwardly against her side, and then he maneuvered her so that she was resting against his chest, one arm draped across his shoulder.

The ground was cold once the surface warmth had been absorbed, but Ivy didn't care. It could have been a sheet of ice.

"All right?" he asked briefly, and that was all. Ivy nodded, forgetting that he couldn't see, but there was no need for words.

Her eyes closed, she inhaled the exciting man-scent of him: leather, wool, and a subtle juniper soap. She was deeply conscious of the strong, steady beat of his heart beneath her ear and she willed her own to a similar rectitude, with little success.

There was no hint of passion in their closeness, nor did she miss it, for in spite of the creeping chill of the evening, she was savoring a warmth that went deeper than mere desire.

After a while a faint breeze sprang up, sending forth a sally of die-hard leaves, and she shivered.

Instantly, Hunter's arms tightened about her. "You're cold," he stated. "What are you wearing, anyway?" He moved her away from him slightly and before she could answer him, he laid a finger across her lips. "No, I'll tell you. Your dark-green corduroy coat—that's easy." His hand slipped under her chin and icy fingers slipped inside the neck of her sweater. "The pink sweater, right?"

"Actually, more of a peach, but how could you tell?"

"The neckline is different from the others." He laughed with a smugness that she found endearing. "Jeans, faded blue with the word 'flower' embroidered across the . . . uh . . . rump, and the dark suede boots with fur inside. Shall I go on?"

Laughter gurgled from her throat as she answered him. "No, please! But how did you know about the jeans? The boots were a logical guess."

"Remember when we came to that fallen log and you helped me get over it without tripping? My hand accidentally brushed across your hip pocket and I felt the design."

"Yes, well, they're a holdover from my high-school days, I'm afraid."

"The distant days of youth, hmm?" He moved his hand to her hair, dislodging the heavy coil and then deliberately removing the hairpins, one by one. "I like it the way you wear it when you go to bed," he confided, the deep rumble of his voice sending strange tremors along her nerves.

"How do you know how I wear it at night?"

"Let's say intuition. One fat braid down your back, right?"

"You cheated! That was how it was on that first morning!" she accused, feeling his body quiver with silent laughter.

The twist of auburn hair was now tumbled over her

shoulder and from there his hands moved on to hold her face between them. "I claim the traditional prerogative of the sightless," he said, letting his sensitive fingers dwell on her cheeks before tracing the line of her nose, her brows, and her mouth. As they touched her lips, she trembled and he pressed lightly, a kiss that left her shaken.

"You're beautiful, you know," he observed unemotionally.

Instinctively backing away from a perilous edge, Ivy disclaimed, "But then, you can't feel the freckles."

"Do you mind them so much?"

"I'm not sure. I've always had them, but it might be nice to have a porcelain-doll look like Evelyn's. Finley always called these my sunspots."

The sun had dropped completely behind the trees now and the air was distinctly cooler. When Hunter spoke again it was to suggest that they start back.

"Evelyn's supposed to call tonight about her plans for the Christmas holidays," he added, moving Ivy away to stand up.

"Oh, yes," she cried brightly, "it's that time again, isn't it? It seems as if we only celebrated Christmas a few weeks ago."

"Give me your hand, Ivy," Hunter bade. She was gathering up the picnic things and after switching the canvas bag to her other hand, she took his and they started up the path. Behind them she could hear the gurgle of the waters as they rushed past the few remaining pilings on their way to the sea.

Almost as if he had resolved something in his own mind that day, Hunter's attitude toward her changed. He remained as polite as she could have asked, but there was none of the closeness that had sprung up between them from time to time, not even the intimacy of a solid argument.

He announced the next day after their walk that Evelyn and the children would be joining them for

Christmas, and then, as if explaining to himself as much as to Ivy, he went on to say that at first he had not wanted the children to see him this way.

"There's always the possibility that it may be permanent, though, so I decided they may as well get used to it."

Disguising a swift thrust of compassion, Ivy schooled her voice to calmness when she asked if he had spent much time with the two girls.

"No, not really. I haven't known Evelyn all that long, as a matter of fact. She was modeling for a charity affair. HS Engineering was sponsoring it, so I had to attend." A wry grin twisted his mouth. "I'm not all that opposed to watching pretty girls parade in fancy clothes, believe it or not. Anyway, I . . . uh . . . met some of the models afterward. When I asked Evelyn if she'd like to have dinner with me, her sister-in-law, whom I hadn't even noticed, said she'd be glad to keep the girls. She had brought them along to watch their mama do her thing. I haven't really seen much more of them, come to think of it."

"How long ago was that?" Ivy asked, taking advantage of Hunter's unusually confiding mood. They had shared a bottle of Burgundy with the beef birds Ivy had prepared for dinner, which may have accounted for the relaxation of his self-imposed reserve.

"It must have been love at first sight," Ivy prompted, knowing she was being foolish and would suffer for it. The sooner she could stop thinking of Hunter as anything but an employer, the better off she'd be.

"It was almost two months ago," he stated in a slightly defensive tone of voice, "and as for your other observation, I think that's a little impertinent, don't you? Anyway, at my age there are other considerations."

"Such as what, Methuselah?" she dared.

"Such as a homemaker, a hostess . . . someone to remember who to send Christmas cards to and whether or not we owe the Joneses a dinner or they owe us," he replied more or less facetiously.

"Sounds like a lovely arrangement. She'll be fortunate." Her flippancy died before it was born, for she knew she would have given her arm to be in Evelyn's shoes, for whatever reason.   "Well, I just hope the children will like it here." Better than their mother does, at least, she added silently. "I'll dig out the decorations and do a bit of shopping if you'd like."

"Fine. Do whatever you think needs doing. As far as my own gift giving goes, I've decided to wait until I can get around a little better."

"Just think, next Christmas you'll have someone else to do it all for you," Ivy commented brightly.

"So I will, so I will," he said, but to Ivy's ears, there was something lacking. The words had a hollow ring.

They went their separate ways as much as possible during the intervening days. Hunter spent more time than he should have in the library working to the limits his handicap allowed while Ivy shopped, baked, and decorated the house with the shabby ornaments on hand, augmented by fresh candy canes and candles. She was hanging a wreath around the newel post when she pierced her finger on the end of a wire and Hunter happened to emerge from the hall in time to hear her muffled, "Darn!"

"What is it?"

"Oh, nothing. I just hurt my finger. I'll live," she told him, gathering up the trimmings and sweeping them into a paper bag.

"Let's see," he ordered, reaching for her hand.

"I told you, it's nothing," Ivy laughed, wondering how he hoped to explore a tiny prick in her finger under the circumstances.

He took her hand and rubbed the back slowly, turning it to run his fingers along her own. "Your hands didn't always feel like that," he observed absently, caressing the palm now in a way that sent small shivers along her spine.

"I didn't always hang laundry out in freezing weather," she retorted with a nervous laugh.

"Can't we get a dryer for you? Why don't you pick one out and have it delivered. Call it a Christmas gift."

"Hunter! Don't be silly! We can't do that—besides, you won't be here much longer. It would be a waste."

"Well, isn't there somewhere you could have the stuff done?"

"Not unless I take it to town and do it myself. That's foolish when I have a perfectly good washer right here."

"Ivy," he said hesitantly, curling her fingers in her palm and tucking her fist under his arm, "you don't have to go. I mean, you could stay here if you want to."

"Oh, but that's impossible!" she exclaimed, shocked.

"Why is it impossible?"

She turned away from him, almost as if afraid he could read her face. "It just is," she replied weakly.

"Where will you go? What will you do?"

"Oh . . . I don't know! Look, do we have to settle my whole future right now? Can it wait until I get the rest of the decorations up?" she cried a little wildly.

"Sorry. It's none of my business, of course," he said shortly, dropping her hand to return to the library.

Evelyn called from Friendship Airport to announce her arrival two full days ahead of schedule. Hunter had arranged for her to be picked up and brought to Rougemont after learning that, due to the holidays, she was unable to book a flight into the closer Smith-Reynolds. Now he was forced to change the arrangements at the last minute. He asked Ivy, while holding a hand over the receiver, if she would take the Jensen to fetch them but Ivy backed away, protesting.

"Oh, no, Hunter, no! I'll be glad to take the jeep, but not your car. I wouldn't know how to drive it. I might . . ."

"Oh, for heaven's sake," he exclaimed impatiently.

"Evelyn," he turned to the receiver again, "would you and the children consider riding in the jeep?"

Ivy could hear the strident protests as far away as she was.

It was finally decided that Evelyn should rent a car and Hunter would pick up the tab. He gave her explicit instructions for finding the place, even though she had been to Rougemont before. Ivy questioned this after he hung up.

"I wouldn't have expected her to pay any attention to landmarks when Bill drove. Women don't, you know—part of the reason she needs someone to look after her."

Ivy stormed away, furious that he couldn't see her anger. Of all the—she hated the expression, but it fit perfectly—male chauvinist pigs!

She went out to the kitchen to parlay a meal for two into something that would feed five. The children might not eat too much, but they'd enjoy something a little festive. She had baked two fruit cakes and a batch of decorated cookies, tentatively planning to bake more later on with the girls' help. She remembered vividly how she had loved helping Mattie make Christmas cookies.

As she dashed around putting last-minute touches on the decorations during the time it took for them to drive from the airport, Ivy told herself it was a good thing the Carlins were descending en masse. A quiet Christmas with Hunter alone, or even with Hunter and Evelyn, might stretch her tolerance too far. It was a poignant enough time at best, for she had so many memories of past Christmases when Granddaddy, Grandmama, and Finley were on hand to help celebrate. Now, knowing her feelings to be so deeply involved—so deeply and so unwisely—it was a good thing her time would be taken up with two small children. That way, perhaps she could forget that Hunter's and Evelyn's marriage was only two months away.

She was tucking extra candy canes into the slightly shabby wreath on the front porch when the late-model sedan drove up and she turned with a wide smile to welcome the children. As if he, too, had been waiting, Hunter emerged from the hall to stand beside her in the sharp, clear air.

"Darling! At last! I thought I'd never get here!" Evelyn cried out, extending a long, exquisitely formed leg as she gracefully extricated herself from behind the wheel.

Ivy looked behind her and then into the backseat but there were no small, wriggling bodies to be seen.

"Get my bags, will you, Ivy?" Evelyn asked, dashing past her to throw her arms about Hunter's neck. "Oh, darling, what a beastly trip! The plane was simply thronged and all I could get was a seat in tourist class. What a crush! You just couldn't *breathe!*"

"The children?" Hunter asked, holding her away slightly and tilting his head in a listening manner.

"Oh, Margaret took them, thank goodness. I didn't know what to do until she offered, because I knew you wouldn't want them cluttering up the place. After all, in your condition . . ." She broke off, slightly discomfited. "I mean, of course, I wanted them, but I was thinking only of you," she added uncertainly.

Ivy was struggling under the burden of two heavy suitcases and a fur coat that had fallen to the floor of the backseat. She was disappointed that the children had not come, but she rationalized that perhaps, after all, it might not be too pleasant to see Hunter in a family-type setting, with children climbing all over him to remind her forcefully that soon, there might be other children, his and Evelyn's . . . no, that might have been too painful to see.

"But, Evelyn, you can't mean to leave them with a stranger over Christmas!" Hunter protested. "And anyway, I thought your baby-sitter was named Grace."

"Oh, Margaret's no stranger, she's Henry's niece.

Alma's child. She and her husband have this enormous place out past Chamblee where the girls positively run wild. It takes me a month to civilize them after they've been there awhile, but it's worth it!"

"Yes, I suppose it is. . . . They must enjoy it, but all the same . . ."

Ivy had an idea that was not exactly what Evelyn had meant, but she continued on upstairs with the bags and opened the room Evelyn had used on her earlier visits. At least this time, she thought with a malicious sort of satisfaction, there'd be no quick, easy trips between adjoining rooms.

Hunter had decided they'd wait and exchange gifts when he could once more see, but of course, Ivy had shopped for the children. Looking pathetic under the tree the day after Christmas were two dolls and several mysterious packages, all paid for by Hunter and selected and wrapped by Ivy.

Evelyn seemed slightly put out by this arrangement. She had brought a pipe for Hunter, who did not smoke, and a book on the history of Atlanta, a lavishly illustrated coffee-table book. Ivy was astounded at the insensitivity of the woman. She watched with open amazement as Evelyn first registered dismay at her gaffe, then quickly turned it into an act of faith.

"I know you can't enjoy it now, darling, but you see, I'm so certain you'll be all right . . . I mean, that your eyes will . . . well, I just decided to prove to you how much faith I have." She beamed as if he could see her and Ivy barely managed to stifle a grunt of disgust.

"The necklace that matches my ring is still available," Evelyn said silkily, then, turning to Ivy, she extended her hand. "You did see this, didn't you, Ivy? Hunter gave it to me the first time he asked me to marry him, but, of course, a girl never says yes the first time, so I wore it on my right hand until I decided to give him the answer he wanted. But you remember, don't you? It was right here at Rougemont and you

and Bill were having a tête-à-tête when I got back. You
looked so guilty when I walked in on you, I couldn't
imagine what you'd been up to, but I was so happy I
decided not to tattle on you to the boss. After all, when
romance is in the air, who knows who may catch the
bug?"

Ivy could have killed her! Hunter's face was flushed
uncomfortably and she saw his fists clenched tightly on
his thighs, as if it tore him apart to hear her making
light of their private affairs.

"I think you're mistaken, Evelyn," he said stiffly.
"Ivy's affections are already engaged in another direction. Anyway, Bill's old enough to be her father."

"He's not that much older than you are, darling, but
of course, Ivy's another generation entirely." Then, as
if brightly determined to change the subject, "I hope
the girls aren't pestering Margaret. If they wear out
their welcome too soon, I won't be able to see the new
year in with you, darling."

It had been Hunter who called the children on
Christmas morning. He located the number from
information, for Evelyn was still upstairs, and placed
the call about the middle of the day. Ivy hovered in the
doorway until they were connected and when Hunter
extended an arm to her, she walked into it without
thinking, as if she were a homing pigeon.

"Hello, Margaret Harvey? This is Hunter Smith—
Evelyn's friend—fiancé. I understand you have the girls
there with you and I thought it would be nice to wish
them a merry Christmas. They are? That's great!"

Ivy listened, her heart a warm lump in her throat, as
he spoke to each girl in turn, listening to a recital of
what Santa had brought and what they had been doing
since they had arrived at the farm. Finally, grinning
down at Ivy, he interrupted to ask if they'd like to
speak to their mother to wish her a merry Christmas.

There was a pause and his arm dropped away,
leaving a penetrating coldness in its stead. "Well, yes,
maybe you're right. Mother's still sleeping, I expect

and . . . yes, she does, doesn't she? Well, she asked me to wish you both a happy Christmas and to tell you she could hardly wait to be with you again.''

He listened again and Ivy could hear the piping childish voices as she watched the grimness come over Hunter's face.

"Yes, sweethearts, you, too. Good-bye now."

He hung up slowly and stood there several moments while Ivy watched apprehensively. Finally, seeming to collect himself, he suggested she must have something to do in the kitchen.

"I certainly do," she snapped, marching away with a hurt flounce that was wasted on him.

That night Ivy went upstairs early, unwilling to play chaperon. She considered calling Finley to wish him a belated merry Christmas, then, remembering Micki, decided he wouldn't be in anyway. She dismissed the idea of calling her father; the card she had received with a picture of Frederick and his family had contained only the usual greeting, written in Louise's handwriting, and there was nothing to indicate that a call from her would be appreciated. She rearranged her bureau drawers, congratulating herself on having trimmed down her possessions to the point where they could be contained in two suitcases.

But it was still early, too early to go to sleep, for there was a restlessness possessing her lately that would not let her relax. Hearing music from the living room, she decided that she could safely slip downstairs and locate a book in the library without disturbing the others. She slipped her feet into soft-soled slippers and pulled on her quilted robe. The night was crystal clear and the temperature was well below freezing outside already, to which the protesting creakings of aged timbers bore witness. Her own room was none too comfortable, either, for in a house originally designed to be heated by fireplaces, the conversion was not always successful. If Hunter hadn't made such a shambles of the library, she could have curled up down there with her book, but it made her secretary's fingers itch every time she saw the place and he had forbidden her to mess with anything on his desk.

Having located a copy of Cantor's *Spirit Lake*, a book she had read years ago and had long intended to reread, she was at the door when voices just outside halted her.

If she had had the good sense to make known her presence immediately, it would not have been quite so embarrassing, but she had automatically checked her steps when she heard Evelyn's usually husky voice shrill with anger and now it was too late.

"I can't understand what's with you, Hunter! Why should you assume I'd bring them? I've never had them underfoot when I could help it, have I? Give me credit for a little common sense! How many men want to be reminded that the woman they plan to marry has had another man in her life, not to mention two noisy reminders of it? Are you a masochist or something that you keep wanting me to bring the kids along wherever we go?" She hardly paused for breath before she was off again. "Hunter, sometimes I think you want the children even more than you do me. Is it that deprived childhood of yours that's working on you? Because if you had me pictured as the domestic little homebody with a clutch of whining kids hanging on to my skirts, you can just forget it. You know what I am . . . and in case you might have forgotten, it's something you seemed eager enough to get your hands on not too long ago. I seem to remember your telling me about places where the nights were warm enough for us to swim bare in the moonlight, and where we could enjoy the privacy of a ski lodge with a roaring fireplace and no one at all to interrupt us. Where do the kids come into a picture like that?"

"Evelyn . . ." he hesitated and Ivy could hear the

tight control he kept over his emotions. "I also seem to
remember your telling me what a bad time you had had
trying to make a home for the girls after Henry died. I
wanted to help . . . I still do. It's not right for you to
have to choose between your husband and your
children. They need all the reassurance they can get
now that they've lost their father and I fully intend to
make it up to them if they'll let me. Believe me, I don't
begrudge them a single minute and I'm more than
ready to help make up for their loss."

"It's my loss you need to make up for, darling." The
husky note was back and Ivy grimaced behind the
library door. "How am I supposed to manage without a
man in my life? All alone in those empty rooms . . .
why couldn't you have done this thing somewhere I
could be with you?"

"You're not alone, my dear. You have the girls and
there's Grace and your sister-in-law. She lives in the
next block, doesn't she?"

"Oh! If you think I want to spend my time swap-
ping recipes and making quaint little mushroom
plaques for the PTA bazaar, you're crazy! I want to
travel, Hunt, and you promised . . ."

The voices faded as they moved on down the hall to
Hunter's bedroom and Ivy's spirits plunged.

Couldn't they wait? She climbed the stairs heavily,
her book forgotten. Why should she be so surprised.
They were engaged, after all, and Hunter was certainly no saint, for all the odd strain of old-
fashioned morality she sometimes sensed beneath the
hard, cynical exterior. Hadn't he told her how difficult it was to have his lover so far away? He had
even tried to assuage his lonely frustration with her, Ivy
reminded herself with painful clarity.

Within five minutes after she had climbed into bed
and pulled the down-filled crazy quilt over her she
heard Evelyn's high-heeled shoes clattering up the
stairs and the door to her room shut with a resounding

bang. A hard core of ice melted somewhere inside her. She went to sleep with a smile on her face.

Two days later Margaret called to say that Kathy had fallen from Oliver Harvey's tractor and cut her leg and that while everything was perfectly all right now, they had had to take several stitches. Evelyn was furious, raging against a fate that would not allow her a single uninterrupted vacation, so Hunter took the phone to ask several succinct questions before satisfying himself that there was no danger of complications.

Evelyn, her thin arms wrapped around her body, shoulders hunched, was pacing back and forth angrily, her high heels clicking as she left the rug for the polished wooden floor. Her beauty was stunning as she turned to confront Hunter, all swirling burgundy skirts and slithering black hair.

"I suppose you think I should rush to her bed-side and do the tear-drenched maternal bit," she demanded, obsidian eyes glittering furiously.

"What I think has nothing to do with it, Evelyn. Margaret has assured me that the cut's not serious. The child tumbled over a disc harrow, but the thing's been properly seen to, tetanus and all that, and I don't think you need worry about infection. She was more frightened than hurt, I imagine."

"Oh, you know so much about children, don't you? Tell me, Hunter, would you have asked me to marry you if I had been single instead of a widow with two dependents?"

"The question doesn't arise, Evelyn," Hunter replied evenly. "You *are* a widow with two dependents."

"Aren't you the Galahad! What am I supposed to do with them while we go trailing all over the world? You promised me we'd travel together, don't forget. Well, what fun do you think I'd have, trailing those two along with me?"

"I think you're more upset than you know, Evelyn,"

Hunter told her impassively. "Perhaps you'd better go lie down for a while."

I just wish they'd have their battles in the privacy of the library, Ivy thought, slamming the silverware drawer in the cherry sideboard. She had been setting the table for lunch and it pained her to be shown so clearly what an absolute hell Hunter had arranged for himself.

When he joined her a few moments later, his hand was massaging the back of his neck and he looked infinitely weary. As Ivy went to return to the kitchen, he turned and she was afraid he meant to follow her, which would not do at the moment. Rinny, a sporadic visitor, had turned up again and was in the kitchen by the stove. The poor old hound had no more idea of obedience than a jackdaw, and it wasn't always easy to budge him once he had found a comfortable spot.

"Do you suppose we might walk down by the river, Ivy?" Hunter asked now, touching the table and easing himself into the chair at the head. He seldom made an error of judgment where movement was concerned, but Ivy was in constant fear that he'd blunder badly and hurt himself. Although the biggest hurt would be to his overweening pride, she had no doubt.

"Walk?" she asked now, transferring her gaze to the window where the sun shone with a brassy glare outside.

"I need some fresh air and I obviously can't do it alone," he replied tersely.

And you wouldn't consider letting Evelyn take you, she thought bitterly, in case your uncanny perception fails you for once and you make a fool of yourself.

"Just let me turn down the oven and grab a coat," she said aloud, hastily rearranging her schedule.

"I'll let Evelyn know," he muttered. "She's gone up to lie down for a while."

On the verge of offering to run upstairs and tell the older woman herself, Ivy reconsidered. She had an idea

Mrs. Carlin would not welcome the news that her fiancé was going for a stroll with the hired help and she didn't particularly want to invite the vituperative comments she might draw. Besides, that would give her time to get rid of Rinny, in case he decided to follow them. He'd be disastrous, dashing back and forth as he usually did when he followed Ivy to the shed.

With the dog shut up in the shed with a succulent soup bone, Ivy hurried back and met Hunter as he opened the back door. His territory was expanding, it seemed, and she'd have to watch out.

"It smells like snow," she told him breathlessly, taking his arm to guide him down the two steps. "Granddaddy always used to make me furious telling me it was too cold to snow. It never made any sort of sense to me." She laughed, and they went on to discuss the weather almost as if they were casual acquaintances who happened to meet on the sidewalk.

She checked his stride when they came to the fallen log and as she guided him over it, Ivy could not help but recall the last time they had come this way. It had been the day they picnicked by the boat house and he had described to her what she was wearing. How could a man be so uncannily perceptive about some things and so obtuse about others?

Twice, Hunter raised his head and told her where they were, describing a distinctive tree or rocky outcropping. He heard the subtle sound of the river long before she did, and when she complained of his usurping her duties, he said, almost wistfully, "I wish you could have taken me to see your quiet waters before I put on my blinders. I've visualized it more than once, but it lacks something."

"We could go there now, I suppose, but the path is all grown up and you wouldn't be able to . . . well, to see it even then."

"You hesitate before the word 'see,' Ivy. Don't treat me with kid gloves. What I'm undergoing is a treatment and only a treatment and there's no reason to tiptoe around so cautiously. I'll leave it up to you whether or not we go visit your private beach."

"It's hardly that." She laughed. "When I think of the beach my mother grew up on, with miles and miles of pink sand and the Atlantic rolling practically up to the front door, this quiet spot on the little Yadkin may not look like much, but it has a charm, all the same. I used to sit there and think that the very water that flowed by my feet would go on to the Scott Reservoir and on into the Pee Dee in South Carolina and then on out into the ocean. It was childish, I guess . . . I never went so far as to launch a note in a bottle, but all the same, it made me seem closer to my mother's people."

"You've visited them? Your mother's folks, I mean."

"Once, but they were living with a cousin then and there wasn't room for me. I think they blamed me, just as my daddy did, for my mother's death. She left them when she discovered she was expecting me because Daddy was at sea and she wanted to be close to his home, his people. If she'd only known how very little that home meant to him, I might have been born on Hatteras instead of here at Rougemont. Funny, isn't it, how a chance decision can influence the rest of your life?"

Hunter was silent for so long, Ivy threw him a curious glance. They were standing at the crest of a small hill that sloped down to the river and against the background of dense pines and cedars, he looked so still that Ivy was somehow sure if she could have seen his eyes, they'd be focused on something far away.

"Would you like to try it?" she asked softly, reluctant to break in on his private thoughts.

"Is it feasible? I don't need a broken neck to go along with my other handicap," he announced with a wry grin.

"Well, there's a place where a spring crosses the path and it's always sort of slippery, as well as a bit steep.

Then there are the vines—honeysuckle and briars—
they make it difficult part of the way. No one has used it
as far as I know since Fin and I used to come down
here."

He turned away and put a tentative foot on the path
that led back up the hill to Rougemont. "In that case, I
think I'll let you preserve the sanctity of your little
shrine. No point in asking for trouble, is there?
Ready?" He extended her a hand and Ivy took it, biting
back the disappointment she felt at the abortive end to
their outing.

"Evelyn should be waking pretty soon anyway, and
she'll want a bit of company. Tomorrow is her last day,
by the way, so perhaps you could manage something
special for dinner tonight. There's a bottle of Musigny
Mommessin '67 that definitely does not call for leftover
turkey."

"It's a little late for thawing something, but I'll see
what I can manage," Ivy replied dully. She made up
her mind to develop a headache that would preclude
her joining them.

"Do you suppose you might want to eat in the
kitchen tonight?" Hunter asked blandly, causing her
hand to tighten convulsively on his arm. "I think that
vintage calls for a candlelight meal for two, don't you?"

Tension seemed to grow by the minute after they
reached the house. Ivy busied herself in the kitchen,
choosing to stay out of the way after consulting Hunter
over a menu for dinner. He had been seated in the large
wing-backed chair and he stood when she came into the
room. She thought for a minute he had taken her for
Evelyn but he dispelled that notion.

"Ivy? I wasn't really serious about your not joining
us for dinner," he said rather hesitantly. "Allow me an
invalid's right to an occasional spot of temperament?"

"I'll allow you anything you wish, Mr. Smith. After
all, you're my employer. Now, if the T-bones will do,

there are two of them in the freezer. I can stuff potatoes and do a spinach salad. Not very exotic, I'm afraid, but then my cooking is strictly country variety."

"I take it I'm not forgiven."

"There's nothing at all to forgive, Mr. Smith. Will that be satisfactory? Oh, and I'll do a rum sauce for the cake."

"If I could be certain of bringing it off without breaking both our necks, *Miss* de Coursey, I'd turn you over my knee," he told her, relaxing back into his chair. "Carry on."

She looked at him suspiciously. There was a hint of a humorous twist to his mouth, but without seeing his eyes, she could not gauge his temper. She was not ready to let him off the hook so easily, anyway, not with Evelyn pacing restlessly in her room and slamming drawers shut as she packed her bags. While the older woman held her tongue whenever Hunter was about, Ivy was a target for her venomous looks and she was not in the mood tonight to sit meekly at the table with them, listening to Evelyn's description of the fabulous wardrobe she was putting together for their honeymoon and the trips she planned to take with Hunter when he resumed his business.

Her head really was beginning to ache when, after clearing the table and putting the dishes in to soak, she was summoned to the living room to have coffee with the other two.

"I thought you might pack up the toys we bought for Amy and Kathy, Ivy, so Evelyn can take them with her tomorrow. Can you find a box that won't be hard to manage on the plane?"

She sipped her coffee, seated on the edge of a chair. "I think so. Maybe they'd fit into one of your suit-cases?" She looked at Evelyn, her eyebrows arched questioningly.

"I don't propose to crush my dresses, thanks. Find something I can check along with my bags."

Long before Ivy was finished with her coffee, Evelyn

was tapping long, silver nails nervously on the alabaster box beside her and casting sulky looks at Hunter, who stood before the radio fiddling with the dials. He selected a Mozart concerto. Its measured perfection only added to the brittle atmosphere in the room.

"I'll locate a box and get them ready for you," she promised, "and now, if you'll excuse me, I still have the dishes to do before I go up to bed."

"The steak was cooked to perfection, Ivy," Hunter said quietly. "Thanks."

"I'm glad."

"Anything would be a relief after all that turkey," Evelyn said disparagingly, and Ivy left the room, taking the coffee things with her. She had had a turkey wing, herself, for dinner, and on the whole, she agreed with Evelyn's verdict.

"Rinny, you're a smart pup," she whispered minutes later, pouring a pan of milk for the dog. "The company is much more pleasant here in the kitchen, so we'll just have a quiet celebration all by ourselves, shall we? It's New Year's Eve, my love; did you know that?"

Her answer was a solid thump of a tail and an adoring gaze, and she pulled a chair across the linoleum and sat down, resting her feet on the edge of the basket where the old hound lay curled up, drowsing.

"Drink your milk, you ingrate. You're too full of turkey broth to move, aren't you? Well, take it easy for a few more minutes, then you'll have to settle for the shed or trot on down to Irma's house."

She let her mind wander, listening to the familiar noises of the old house. The clock in the hall wheezed, then struck the hour, and reluctantly she stirred. Mozart had given way to something harsh and discordant and she heard Hunter's voice as he said something to Evelyn. He seemed to be headed this way so she urged the dog out of his comfortable bed. "Come on, darling, you'll have to go, now. Up you get. It would never do to have you discovered here, my sweet, because that would be the end of everything."

She supposed she really should confess her misdemeanor to Hunter, but it pleased her, somehow, to have this small secret indulgence. She doubted if, for all his occasional kindness, he would tolerate such a miserable excuse for a dog in his kitchen, much less in the rest of the house.

The animal stood and stretched, his ungainly limbs splaying out awkwardly as he tilted his massive head on one side as if to ask if she was sure he had to go.

"Yes, you have to go, sweetheart." She laughed. "Now, come on, be a good boy and I'll slip you back in tomorrow night, hmmm?"

She opened the back door and let the dog amble reluctantly past her; before closing it, she sniffed the clear, cold air. It really *did* smell like snow, she decided. Shivering, she closed the door quietly and crossed the room to switch out the lights.

Before her hand had touched the pull chain that hung from the old-fashioned fixture in the middle of the room, she heard Hunter's bedroom door slam.

Things must have deteriorated rapidly after she left the room, she decided with a shrug. She stifled a yawn, turned out the light, and entered the hall where she was accosted by Evelyn.

"What happened to Hunt?" the other woman asked.

"How should I know?" Ivy returned, not particularly graciously but too tired at the moment to care.

"He insisted on inviting you to join us for a midnight toast and next thing I know, he's slammed his door like a nasty-tempered little boy."

"Sorry. I didn't even see him. If he's upset, then it's nothing to do with me."

Evelyn tapped her foot impatiently. "I must say, he's been nervy lately. I really don't envy you your position if this is the way he usually acts."

Ivy neither confirmed nor denied Hunter's behavior as she climbed the stairs to her room. His moods were a mystery to her and it was all she could do to keep out of his way when, for no reason at all, he seemed to revert to his normal ill humor. It made the times like today, when he had stood with an arm draped casually across her shoulders and described to her the rock formation and the trees along the riverbank from memory, all the more incomprehensible.

Chapter Six

The promised snow fell and Rougemont took on that slightly depressing feeling that occurred when the snow glare from outside showed up every speck of dust and each scratch on the well-used old furniture. If Ivy had prided herself on her care of the place, her pride took a fall; she decided that before her time was up, she must see that each room had a thorough turning out, even if it meant staying on after Hunter's treatment was finished. She could always ask Irma, Mattie's daughter, to help out with the heavy work.

Hunter had gone back to his old habit of working most of the morning and, several times, the afternoons as well, and Ivy thought despairingly of Bill's misplaced trust in her ability to make him rest. On the few occasions she had dared mention it to him, he had seared her with an arctic blast of temper.

Rinny turned up with a friend one day and Ivy

decided she was going to have to put an end to her philanthropy, for when she left, there'd be no one to care for the dogs, unless Irma agreed to take them on. She was growing attached to Rinny, for all his vagrant ways, but she certainly couldn't take him with her when she left, for she had no idea where she would be going.

One morning during the second week of January, Hunter asked her to join him in the library after she finished her morning chores. He must have sensed her surprise, natural enough, considering he practically threatened her life whenever she suggested she might clean up the place for him.

"You said you were a secretary, didn't you? Typing speed up, accuracy all it should be?"

"Yes. I never had any complaints, that is," she replied cautiously, wary of something she sensed in his manner.

"Would you consider doing some typing for me?"

She relaxed a bit. "Of course."

"There's no of course about it. You were hired as a housekeeper and you're under no obligation to help out in any other capacity."

Recalling the times when he had taunted her with the promised bonus that was to buy her complete services for three months, she remained silent.

In the end, she agreed to join him in the library, or the office as he preferred to call it lately, after she had done the dishes and the beds. As she hurried through a sketchy cleanup in the kitchen, she found herself growing oddly tense. They had resumed the impersonal relationship of employer-employee since the first of the year and Ivy was not sure she wanted to commit herself to spending more time closed up in the fairly small library with him.

She absently hung up his clothes; Hunter made no pretense at picking up after himself, nor did she expect him to. She held a chamois shirt in her arms, smoothing it with her hand as she inhaled the combined scents of after-shave and his own body, then, chiding herself for her foolish daydreaming, she hung it in the wardrobe and closed the door with a firm click. She made his bed with speed and efficiency, not allowing her hands to linger over the task, and then, when she was done, she stood in the doorway and surveyed the room.

There was an almost monklike austerity about it, for it held nothing except the double bed, the ungainly wardrobe, and one straight chair, but Hunter rejected her offer to bring in a more comfortable one, saying he didn't need anything else to stumble over.

If she had held doubts about the wisdom of allowing herself to spend hours in close proximity with Hunter, they were quickly dispelled. She was set the task of transcribing tapes he had made of various reports, meetings, and specifications while Hunter, himself, turned his back in the tilted chair and donned a headset to listen to still more tapes from the batch that came almost daily from Atlanta.

The phone rang periodically and Ivy answered, tapping him on the shoulder and handing him the receiver. There were surprisingly few words spoken between them that first week and Ivy was not sure whether she was relieved or disappointed.

Nights, after dinner, she took to spending more time in the library transcribing more tapes, having once caught on to the technique. She was slow at first, but Hunter seemed not to be in any particular hurry and gradually she made inroads on the pile that had accumulated since he had first begun receiving them.

It served to excuse her from having to share the living room with him, at any rate. Sitting before the fire listening to the news broadcasts followed by whatever music Hunter selected had a way of making her edgy although she didn't try to hide from herself the fact that she was missing the former closeness they had shared.

Hunter had a single whiskey each night and Ivy had an occasional sherry, but she was glad to have a reason to take it in the library.

One night he switched off the radio in the middle of Beethoven's Fourth Symphony and came to stand in the door as she was rewinding a taped report of a sales conference. She looked up to see more than the usual amount of tension on his face.

"Are you all right?" she asked impulsively.

"Did Bill leave you anything for headaches?"

"Yes, he did," she told him, flipping the switch on the recorder and standing. "Do you need something?"

"If you don't mind."

She had put the medicines, both of them, in her own bathroom for safekeeping and now she excused herself and dashed upstairs to return moments later with the small bottle of capsules.

"I'll get you some water. Just a minute."

He was back in the living room when she returned with a glass of water and the prescribed dose and she held out the glass and watched as he downed the dose.

Instead of allowing her to take the glass from him when she held out her hand for it, Hunter closed his hand over her wrist and placed her hand on his forehead.

"That feels good," he sighed. "Your hands are cool."

With no conscious decision, Ivy remained behind his chair, her hands working gently on his brow to soothe away the furrows. She heard him take a deep breath, almost as if he had finally reached a state of peace—which was a bit of high-flown fancy on her part, she thought derisively.

Her hands worked themselves down his neck to his shoulders and she felt the tension gathered there. He leaned forward after a while and she was able to reach the rock-hard muscles of his upper shoulders, lifting and kneading, until she felt some of the tightness go.

It was Hunter who called a halt. Ivy could have

remained indefinitely, savoring the touch of his flesh, even under such circumstances as these.

"You'd better go up, Ivy," he said tiredly. "You've done two days' work and I can't ask you to start a third at this late hour."

"I don't mind. The office work is a break from the housekeeping and vice versa."

Her fingers left his back reluctantly and she paused before leaving the room to look back. He sat where she had left him, his head resting on his hand, which was braced against the wing of the chair. He looked so tired, so . . . helpless, she thought with surprise. Somehow, that was the last word she would have thought to use to describe Hunter Smith.

The next morning there was no sign of the previous night's weakness. He strode into the breakfast room as if daring the chair to be one quarter of an inch out of position when he dropped down into it.

He made short work of breakfast and was hard at it when Ivy finally joined him in the library.

"Headache all gone?" she asked, more to announce her presence than anything else, for there was no sign of last night's discomfort on his face.

"Yes. Clear this mess away, will you?" he indicated a sacrosanct pile of folders she had been forced to work around for days. "Until they start sending these damned reports in Braille, they may as well save the postage. Now, what are you working on?"

"I was transcribing a tape between you and McGivens about—"

"I know what it's about! Put that aside and take a letter."

She did as he demanded, her shorthand barely up to the speed at which he dictated. He usually showed more concern for her only adequate ability, but today something was definitely out of kilter.

"Shall I get this off today, sir?" she asked when he finally stopped dictating and swiveled his chair away from her.

"Are we back to the 'sir' stage again or is that just a reaction to the office setting?"

"A reaction, I think . . . sir." She added the last word with a decided gleam in her eye, not that he could see it.

"The perfect secretary," he mused. "I wonder how the perfect secretary would react if her boss asked her to take a personal letter."

"I'm sure the perfect secretary would take it in her stride, sir," Ivy retorted meekly, her eyes dwelling on the broad shoulders that appeared above the back of the chair before her.

"In that case, shall we test it?"

Ivy had only a moment to ponder the peculiar note in his voice as she sat, pencil poised over her notebook, before he began to speak.

"Dearest," he began. "Would you prefer that to say, my darling? Or perhaps you have a favorite greeting?"

"What about dear sir?"

"I hardly think she'd appreciate that," he grinned, swinging his chair around to the desk. "Stick to dearest. Let's see. . . . How's this? The distance between us is fast becoming untenable. What am I to do when I find myself unable to touch you, to hold your body in my arms and feel your heart pounding in rhythm with my own?"

The teasing note was gone and his voice had taken on a deeper note, causing Ivy to stare at him in consternation.

"I can't write that," she gasped in a strangled voice.

"Why not?"

"Because . . . because it's just not right for one woman to know what's in a letter of that sort . . . when it's written to another woman, that is."

"They're only words. What if I were a novelist? Would that make the words more acceptable?"

"But you're not," she rebuked.

As if tiring of the game, Hunter sighed. "No, I'm not."

Then he went on to tell her that he would no longer need her services as a secretary. "You've been a big help, Ivy, but I think we can keep abreast with maybe a weekly session unless something special comes up. The thing with Varga may break within the next few weeks—the microelectronics fellow, remember? In that case, I may have to call on you again."

Three days later the snow melted enough so she decided to go into Wilkesboro for supplies.

"If that means we'll no longer be eating the redoubtable ham, I'm all for it. I thought it was going to last as long as that turkey did," Hunter informed her, pushing his coffee cup across the table for a refill.

"Sorry about that . . . sir."

"Hunter."

"What?"

"I said Hunter. You're no longer my secretary so you can cut the sir. As long as I have to be shut up here with no outside contacts, I'd prefer to be called by my given name in case I forget who I am."

"Yes, Hunter," Ivy replied with false meekness. "Not that I think you're in any danger of forgetting who you are. You probably have more people working for you than I've met in my whole lifetime and from the calls I've taken for you, they all think of you as The Mr. Smith, capitalized, written in gold letters in a flamboyant style."

"I'm fairly certain that each and every one of the several million Smiths considers himself The Mr. Smith," Hunter said drily.

"But then, they don't know the *real* Mr. Smith, do they?"

"Are you being impertinent?"

Answering his grin with one of her own, she denied the charge.

"One of these days I'm going to take you down a peg or two," he promised, with a return to the good humor Ivy thought was little more than a memory.

Three days later, Ivy was bringing in a load of firewood from the stack out by the twin oaks to the shelter of the back porch when she was startled to hear Hunter calling her.

"Is something wrong?" she asked, shucking off her work gloves as she hurried toward the back door.

"That we'll soon find out. Can you stop whatever you're doing for a few minutes and come inside?" He stood aside for her to enter and she reached automatically for his arm as she passed, but he brushed her off impatiently and strode across the room, coming perilously close to the corner of the table. He made it to the door with no mishap and she marveled, not for the first time, at the sheer arrogance of the man. Forget the torpedoes, full speed ahead!

Turning to face her in the library, he came right to the point. "Look, I've got to fly south for a few days—four at most—and I obviously can't do it alone. Will you come with me?"

"What?" Her fingers froze in their absent task of securing the hairpins in her fallen chignon.

"Did I somehow fail to make myself clear?" he asked sarcastically. "All I'm asking is that you help me on and off a few jet liners, being sure I don't end up on the wrong continent by mistake. I may ask you to sit in on a meeting or two to handle the taping if no one objects. It will save any possible misunderstanding when negotiations are ended. How long will it take you to pack a bag for each of us?"

"Let me get my breath!" she exclaimed. "Now. We're going south. Atlanta?"

"St. Croix."

"The Virgin Islands?" she crowed, astonished.

"Have you anything in particular against them?"

"I've never even been out of the country. Hardly out of the state." Ivy dropped down onto a chair, still too stunned to take in the sudden change of plans.

"You're not leaving the country even so. Officially, that is. St. Croix is a U.S. possession. So! Here's the drill. We'll leave from Smith-Reynolds on Piedmont, take Eastern from Atlanta and Pan-Am from Miami. There'll be a brief stop at St. Thomas, but that's all. Can we be ready by eleven tonight? That will put us a day ahead of schedule and I can use the time."

For the next few hours, Ivy functioned in a daze. She consulted Hunter about clothes, then had to scramble about to locate her own summer things, such as they were. Jeans, trunks, and a dinner jacket for him, he said, leaving Ivy to fill in the gaps, and she decided on the equivalent for herself; jeans, bikini, a couple of sun dresses, and one dinner dress just in case.

She was ready to leave with half an hour to spare and as an afterthought, she slipped into the library to call Irma Clamrock, Mattie's daughter.

"Irma? This is Ivy. . . . Yes, it has, hasn't it? . . . Oh, is she? That's good. Look, Irma, there's a great big goof of a dog who's . . . yes, that's right. . . . Oh, no! Did he really?"

On learning that Rinny was an accomplished enough panhandler to have at least two homes within a five-mile radius, she ceased worrying about him. The old fake! She grinned, picturing the hangdog, pathetic attitude that had no doubt produced a meal and a good bed on half the farms this side of the Blue Ridge Mountains.

And Mattie was coming home. It would be good to see the old dear, for she had been more or less a fixture of Ivy's childhood. Ivy only hoped her visit had done her "rheumatics" enough good to see her through the winter.

"Aren't you ready yet? Get a move on or we'll miss our flight. We still have to get to Winston-Salem, you know," Hunter urged from the hallway.

The clash came when he handed her his car keys.

"Oh, no, I couldn't," Ivy balked, hands hastily pushed behind her as if to ward off his insistence.

"What the . . . ! Come on, Ivy, I haven't time for any coy games."

"It's no game, Hunter," she protested indignantly. "I could no more drive a car like that than I could fly! Well . . ." Remembering that she was soon to fly for the first time, she hesitated. Then, "No. It's out of the question. All I've ever driven is the old jeep and if that's not good enough for you then you can count me out."

With no time to argue, she won her case. When they pulled into Smith-Reynolds Airport, Ivy grabbed Hunter, while he grabbed the two bags and his briefcase and they made it with minutes to spare.

The hours that followed were out of time and space for Ivy. Hunter quickly discovered that she had never flown before and he held her hand during the takeoff, told her what to expect from her ears, how to cope with it, and prayed audibly that she would not be airsick.

"Who's taking care of whom?" She laughed a little shakily once when they hit an air pocket and he pulled her to him, muttering reassurance against her hair.

Not until the pilot announced that they were landing in Atlanta in twenty minutes did Ivy turn to Hunter in consternation and ask, "What about Evelyn? What will she think if she tries to reach you and nobody answers?"

"She knows the plans. I called before we left home."

"And she didn't mind?"

He turned to her and just as if he had had no blindfold across his eyes, she could read the austere expression. "Whether she minded or not is beside the point. This is strictly a business trip, not the first, nor will it be the last."

So put that in your pipe and smoke it, Ivy thought. Aloud, she said, "All the same, I think if you were my fiancé, I'd feel a little left out."

By the time they swooped in over St. Thomas, Ivy was exhausted, her nerves stretched to the breaking point. She had not been able to sleep, due partly to the excitement of flying, and partly to the enormous sense of responsibility she felt for the man who was sitting so quietly beside her in the first-class compartment of the jet liner.

It had been impossible to miss the interest of several of the women passengers, as well as the stewardess, and Ivy was certain it was no mere curiosity that directed their not-so-subtle stares. Hunter was dressed casually, his dark-blue pullover shirt now open at the neck to reveal the shadow of dark hair, and the pale-gray slacks stretched tightly across his muscular thighs as he slipped down in his seat to try to catch a few winks.

Ivy was glad he could rest, for she had not missed his fingers moving restlessly over his briefcase as if itching to draw out the contents and spread them across his lap. She considered offering to read any pertinent papers to him, but decided against it.

St. Thomas appeared like a scene from a travel poster after hours of flying across empty ocean and when Ivy leaned down to peer through the window as they came in for a landing, Hunter stirred beside her.

"I'd better explain about our accomodations, Ivy."

She turned away from the brilliant, sun-lit spectacle below and sighed. "Yes?" she prompted reluctantly. They had spent hours together during which he might have explained anything he thought she needed to know. Now, when at last there was something to see, he decided to instruct her. "I wish you could see this, Hunter, but of course, it's probably old hat to you. I still can't believe I haven't wandered into a travelog. It's all so—so picturesque!"

She peered out the window again in time to see them bank over a sheer cliff and sweep in toward a mountain and she gasped and clutched his arm.

When he spoke, there was quiet amusement in his voice. "I tried to distract you."

There was a hard, warm hand covering her own, but Ivy was only vaguely aware of it as she waited for the inevitable impact.

"St. Thomas is always a little hairy," he observed. "These mountains were not built with jet traffic in mind."

"You mean you always have to squeeze a landing in between the ocean and the mountain like that?" she asked, astounded.

He shrugged. "Wait till you see St. Croix. I wish there were time to show you some of the other Virgins—Buck Island Underwater Park and Virgin Gorda, perhaps."

"If they all take as many years off my life as this one did, I can do without it, thanks," she remarked drily, gathering up the purse that had fallen to the floor.

"Sit tight. We'll be off again in a few minutes and I promise you no more deeds of derring-do. The St. Croix strip is quite tame."

In the short hop between the islands, Hunter explained that they would be staying with a couple he had known for years.

"You'll like the Orsinis, Pete and Zanne. They set up this meeting with Homer Varga for me, after arranging to have him tour the Puerto Rico Plant. Varga's the microelectronics man I mentioned awhile back, remember? Anyway, I think we might come to a mutually advantageous agreement within a day or so and the sooner we have a contract sewn up, the sooner you can climb into your bikini and sample a little of the Cruzan sunshine."

The taxi drive up from the airport through the weathered flamboyance of Fredericksted and on up the Hamm's Bluff Road took Ivy's breath away. She twisted constantly in her seat, catching tantalizing glimpses of aquamarine water through lush groves of palm trees. The air was redolent with the perfume of hundreds of flowering trees and vines, the likes of which she could not have imagined, and she caught her breath at the sight of poinsettias that were rooftop high.

"Hunter, I think I just saw a poinsettia tree. Am I crazy?"

He laughed and squeezed her hand. "No, honey, you're not. Those little Christmas plants we see in flowerpots at home really take off down here, don't they? I'll have to get Zanne to give you the horticultural tour. I'm not much on flowers and such, but Zanne's a real expert. Pete can fill you in on the local history, too. That's his bag, along with golf and bridge. He's retired now and they built the villa with room enough to entertain all their friends from the States."

"Lucky for us."

The taxi driver deposited them in front of a sprawling pink- and white-stucco building with red Spanish tiles on the roof and an Olympic-size pool in the side patio. The thick walls were all but covered with flowering vines and wherever she looked, Ivy caught fascinating glimpses of glossy, green shrubs and outsized flowers. She paid the man from Hunter's billfold after he had interpreted the Cruzan dialect for her. It was a musical patois that fell delightfully on the ears and she thanked him for taking the bags to the front door for her.

Before she could ring the bell, the door burst open and a tiny, colorful whirlwind swept them up.

"Hunt! Why didn't you call from the airport? I didn't hear the doorbell. Oh, it probably doesn't work, nothing much does around here, but come in, come in!"

Zanne Orsini was like a parakeet, Ivy soon decided. Her hands were never still, her bright black eyes darted constantly, and her exotic, colorful clothes fluttered as she dashed back and forth seeing to the comfort of her guests. There could be no doubt that she ran her home and her large, phlegmatic husband with equal ease, and Ivy quite understood when, on hearing Hunter tease his hostess about her constant birdlike flutterings the next day, Pete spoke up.

"You know how we get the parrot to shut up and go to sleep, don't you? Well, my friend, it works just as well with my flighty little wife. Just turn out the lights and presto!"

"Does the trick, hmmm?" Hunter grinned.

"Quiets her down . . . doesn't always put her to sleep immediately," he quipped, casting a slow wink at his flushed, protesting wife.

Ivy decided she liked them both enormously. Pete regaled her willingly with tales of Arawak and Carib Indians and of the seven flags that had flown over the island from time to time. Zanne sat on the rattan glider, feet tucked beneath her. She sipped a tall rum drink as she listened to Hunter talk of mutual acquaintances.

It was after dinner that Zanne followed Ivy to the lovely, cool guest room and perched brightly on the bed while Ivy repaired her makeup and swept her hair into a more secure bun.

"I could hardly wait to get you alone," the older woman confided.

"Why?" Ivy asked, looking at her curiously in the mirror.

"Well, to tell you how thrilled we were to hear about Hunt's plans, for one thing, and to find out about this eye thing. Just what is the prognosis?"

"It's a treatment, really. Three months of complete rest and he should be as good as new. At least, that's what his doctor told me, and I believe him implicitly."

"I guess you have to, don't you? It would be hell otherwise, feeling the way you do." Zanne studied the girl openly, her bright eyes holding nothing save a warm, friendly curiosity.

"Feeling the way I do?" Ivy repeated in spite of herself. There was a chilled sort of numbness somewhere in her middle that spread rapidly as she heard Zanne's next words.

"Oh, love, it's perfectly obvious, and we think it's the best thing that's happened since we've known him. Hunt's had a rough time coming to terms with himself and I don't mind telling you there were a few real harpies in his past. Pete and I held our breath for fear he'd get caught by one of the predatory witches, because, for all his much-vaunted genius, Hunt's a babe in the woods when it comes to women. That's why, when he told us he was going to bring you along, we jumped at the chance to see for ourselves what sort of woman he had finally fallen for. Well, it was easy to see why he picked you from all the rest, Ivy, and it just makes me feel warm all over to know how crazy about him you are. . . . He deserves the best."

Even if there were any words Ivy could have thought of just then to explain the enormous mistake Zanne had made, she could not have got them past the constriction in her throat. She had turned slowly on the vanity stool to stare in consternation at the other woman, helpless to halt the cheerful babbling voice.

"But I'm not . . . I mean, we're not . . ." she began, only to be stopped in her tracks.

"Just answer me this one thing, Ivy. Do you truly love him?"

Stricken, Ivy could only gaze through the sudden shimmering lights and with a lie on her tongue, she heard herself with horror confessing the secret she had borne for too long alone.

"I love him," she said in a tiny voice.

"Then that's all I can ask. If you can stick to him during this three-month ordeal, you can't be out for a good time like all the others. Honestly, there were times when I think he'd have been better off chucking the whole HS Engineering thing and setting himself up on a research grant somewhere. At least he'd be sure that way that his woman wanted Hunter the man, not just H. E. Smith, the third, and all his worldly assets. That's why I'm glad I caught Pete when he was a poor, struggling economics instructor, before he went to work for private industry and reaped his just rewards. Gives a gal a smug feeling of self-righteousness, doesn't it?"

Ivy had tossed her dinner dress across the foot of the

bed, as Zanne had decreed a meal by the pool after a swim. Now the black- and brown-jersey print seemed to writhe sickeningly before her eyes as she tried to force herself to speak. It was imperative that she clear up this misunderstanding. The embarrassment, otherwise, would be more than she could stand. In fact, it already was.

"Look, Zanne, I'm afraid my position here isn't what you think," she began miserably.

"If you mean I should have given you all a double room instead of a connecting one, that's all right, honey. It just so happens that Pete and I share the only double in the house."

"No! Please . . . just listen, will you?" Ivy cried.

With a funny little moue, Zanne assumed a pose of patience, her head tilted on one side, and Ivy surrendered to a slightly hysterical desire to giggle. "Zanne . . . I'm not Evelyn," she said as if that explained it all.

"Well, no, I didn't think you were," her hostess said sagely. "Only, who's Evelyn?"

"Oooh," Ivy groaned. Then she proceeded to relate the circumstances of her being there, telling about Evelyn Carlin's relationship to Hunter and their plans for the immediate future.

"Yuk! I really put my size three in it, didn't I? Well, what's the verdict?"

At the questioning lift of Ivy's eyebrows, she reiterated, "What's she like, this Evelyn? All Hunt said on the phone was that he was engaged and she was a widow with two small children. I must say, I thought you were either amazingly well preserved or you had got a head start on most of the rest of us. You can't be more than twenty."

"Twenty-two," Ivy confided, hoping the question of her opinion of Evelyn Carlin had passed safely by.

"Hey, are you two coming out again tonight?" Pete called through the door, earning Ivy's eternal gratitude. As little as she thought of the woman Hunter was to marry, it was not up to her to prejudice his friends on her account, nor, she had discovered to her dismay, was she particularly successful at evading the truth.

The next two days were full ones, what with Zanne's determination that Ivy should not miss any of the island's attractions. Ivy protested that she was here to help tape the business meetings, but Zanne brushed aside her protests, delegating the taping to Pete.

"He can push a button now and then without straining himself, the big ox. You've never been to the Caribbean and I'm going to see that you have a ball."

It was impossible to miss the speculative glances they threw at both Ivy and Hunter. Ivy burned with embarrassment at the thought of what she must have told her husband. Still, it was hard to resist the languorous delight of an afternoon spent beside the pool, soaking up enough sun to triple her crop of freckles, or a thrilling walk along a rocky, moonscaped beach with a heavy surf making strange music as it washed over millions of tiny pebbles.

She had been warned about the sea urchins, those spiny creatures that stalked the bottoms looking like some exotic black flower, and she wore a pair of sneakers whenever she darted out into the water to retrieve a particularly colorful pebble. Zanne promised to see that she got to swim in the Caribbean at least once before they had to return.

Finding Hunter alone on the patio with a tall drink in his hand the second evening, Ivy dropped down in the empty chair beside him. She felt terribly guilty about having such a wonderful time while he was closeted all day with the men, but when she expressed her feelings, he made light of them.

"But why on earth did you bring me, if Pete can do whatever you need in the way of note-taking?" she asked, studying the pale, lean face beside her and wishing he had more time to soak up some sun while they were there.

"Believe it or not, I'm not quite up to the task of

getting myself on and off several planes alone. Besides, I find it more fun to travel with a companion." That last was added with a definite teasing note and Ivy retorted in kind.

"Funny, I would never have taken you for the gregarious sort. Maybe you should have signed up for a Cook's Tour."

"Yes, well, that might be stretching it a bit. By the way, Zanne said something about taking you to do a bit of shopping tomorrow while we wind up things here and this might come in handy." He shifted in his seat to reach his billfold and then handed her a thick sheaf of notes with directions to take whatever she needed.

"I can't take that," she gasped.

"Don't be silly. I owe you a month's salary and you'll have a far better time spending it here than you will back home. If you want an advance, feel free."

"No, I won't need to buy much. Unless there's something I could get for you? A gift for Evelyn, maybe, if you'd trust me to select something?"

He drained the last of his drink and sat the glass down accurately on the table beside him. "I don't think so, thanks. Evelyn's made her preferences clear as far as gifts are concerned and I'll be shopping at a certain jewelry store in Atlanta, I guess." He didn't sound particularly enthusiastic about the prospect, but then, that was none of Ivy's concern, she decided.

"I think it would do you good to get some sun while we're here. Zanne's promised to show me a beach where the bottom's safe for swimming, so if you finish up in time tomorrow, maybe you can come along with us," she suggested.

"We'll see."

After several minutes of silence, she spoke again. "Hunter," she said tentatively.

"Hmmm?" He was leaning back in his chair, almost as if he were asleep, and Ivy could not prevent her eyes from straying over his blatantly masculine body. The jeans and black knit shirt hinted at latent power.

"Hunter, I'm awfully afraid I'm not earning my keep. I haven't done a single thing for you since we got here."

"What were you doing a day or so ago when I asked you to come with me?"

Puzzled, she cast her mind back. "I was stacking wood on the back porch in case it rained," she told him.

"And before that?"

"Good heaven . . . I was hanging out the laundry and I forgot to take it in!"

At her tone of voice, he laughed. "You're an absurd little thing, you know that? You earn your keep, Ivy, never fear. It was worth a good deal to me just to hear your comments as we flew in over the islands and then on the drive up here. Sometimes, even with two good eyes, one forgets how to see."

They sat quietly, with Ivy taking in the beauty of hibiscus blooming against a background of mahogany and mango trees and after a while the chorus of tree frogs tuned up, making a deafening counterpoint to the music of Pete's stereo that came through the jalousies.

She slept lightly that night, covered only in the sheet. The house was built with a large square living area in the center and bedrooms and baths along each side. The fact that she and Hunter were the only inhabitants of their particular wing made her nervous, which was strange, considering she had been alone with him in an isolated house for weeks now. Perhaps it was something in the seductive fragrance of the air, or the sibilant whisper of the water washing millions of pebbles against the rocky beach. Then again, it could be the simple fact that she found it all but impossible to think of Evelyn and all the details of daily life back in the States. The geography defeated her; her mind would not stretch.

At any rate, she was awake in an instant when Hunter entered her room and touched her shoulder.

"What is it?" she whispered, sitting up with the sheet

clutched around her as if he could see the sheer nylon gown she was wearing.

"Did you bring the headache caps?"

She gasped in dismay. "Oh, Hunter! I'm afraid I forgot. Is it bad?"

"Not yet," he replied rather grimly, "but if I don't catch it now, it will be and I need to be in top shape for the windup session tomorrow."

"Maybe Zanne would . . ."

"I'd just as soon not bother them. They've been asleep for hours now."

"Well, I could look in the medicine cabinet. There might be some aspirin," she offered hopefully.

"Will you? Thanks. I'll wait in my room."

Slipping out of bed, Ivy padded quietly to the bathroom and closed the door carefully before turning on the light. She had not been able to see whether or not Hunter wore his blindfold but she was not about to take any chances.

There were no aspirin, no medicines of any sort, and Ivy reluctantly let herself into the adjoining room to tell him so. In the slight light from a setting full moon, she saw him sitting up in his bed, kneading the muscles at the back of his neck in the old familiar manner.

With no conscious thought on her part, she found herself standing beside his bed slipping her own cool hands beneath his larger, warmer ones.

"There aren't any, I'm afraid. Does this help any at all?"

"Mmmmm. Keep it up. It certainly doesn't hurt. Here, do this," he murmured, moving her hands to his temples.

She stroked evenly, massaging away the knotted tension and letting her fingers stray across his brow to ease the furrows there, then back to the tight muscles at the back of his neck. Her own body was cramped, for she was forced to lean over at an awkward angle to reach him, but she barely noticed this, so conscious was she of the silky texture of his skin beneath her fingers.

The warm scent of his body arose to her nostrils with a spicy, faintly musky fragrance and her breath quickened.

"You'll break your back," Hunter whispered deeply, capturing her wrist and turning over on his side at the same time. "Here, come in with me and see if that eases you any. It's doing me a world of good, so don't stop, please."

Under the circumstances, she was helpless, but she was deeply aware of the dangers as she slipped under the sheet onto the space already warmed by his body. He wore only a pair of pants and his back was warm against her as she went to work on his knotted muscles again.

It was still not right. "Turn onto your stomach," she whispered, rising to her knees beside him. That made it easier, but she wished she had the nerve to straddle his back so she could really put the pressure behind her hands. Her fingers lifted and smoothed, pounded lightly and kneaded; he felt so relaxed she thought he was going to sleep. That would put an end to his headache.

She eased the weight of her hands, listening for the slow deepening of his breathing that would tell her he was asleep. Instead, she heard a rasping sound and almost simultaneously, she became aware of the pounding of his heart beneath her hands. Before she could escape, he had turned and his hands were on her shoulders, bearing her down so that she fell across his bare chest.

"This is crazy," she muttered, even as his mouth touched hers, capturing her completely. There was no careful buildup, but an immediate deluge of passion that left her helpless as his mouth explored her own, probing sensuously, lifting to nibble at her lower lip before descending once more to drain her will from between her lips.

His hands slipped up under the short nylon gown and stroked her back and her shoulders, causing frissons to make her breath catch in her throat, and her own hands clutched at his shoulders before moving up to tangle in his hair. He lifted his hands and somehow, she found herself on her back with his weight on her, his mouth trailing slowly, torturingly from her eyes to her temples and on to the corners of her mouth, where he probed sensuously with his tongue before capturing her mouth again in a kiss that rocked her to her very soul.

Her gown was up around her neck and his head was on her breasts, his warm breath fanning out against sensitized nipples as he whispered her name over and over, and his own body could not hide the state of his arousal. Faint alarms were sounding in the back of her mind but she was determined to ignore them, tuning out the teaching and instincts of a lifetime as she surrendered to a passion that nothing had ever prepared her for.

It was as he lifted her slightly to pull the gown over her head that Ivy's arm flung out and struck something on the bedside table. With the shattering crash of the carafe on the floor, they both froze. It was Hunter who recovered first. He rolled off her, onto his side, with his back to her, and Ivy caught the faint groan that was forced from him.

"Hunter? Are you all right?"

"No, you little fool! Get out of here while I can still let you go!"

Still she hesitated, sensing his agony, wanting to ease it even as she acknowledged her own aching disappointment. But for that one careless move . . . She touched his back, the skin hot under her fingers, and he flung back a hand that caught her on the side.

"Go, will you? Just go!"

Shivering in the warm night air, she slid from the bed and hurried across the room, scarcely feeling it when she stepped on a piece of broken glass.

She didn't see him before they left for town and the shops, and Ivy could only hope he escaped the broken glass. Her conscience battered her for not returning to clear away the mess before he got out of bed, but she could not bring herself to go back. She did, however, mention to Pete when she came upon him still in pajamas, spilling coffee grounds across the floor in an attempt to open a tin of the stuff, that she had heard glass break in Hunter's room last night and that Pete might want to check it out before anything happened.

She hurried away, not wanting to see the speculative look he cast her. Perhaps he hadn't; it could have been just her overactive imagination that made her think Pete was watching the pair of them with more than a little interest. At any rate, Ivy was in no condition to counter any awkward questions he might pose at that hour of the morning and she was just as glad when Zanne came in to propose they make an early day of it, getting all the shopping done before the shops closed for siesta.

As they whipped down the hill in the little Volvo, with a chattering Zanne behind the wheel, Ivy tried to keep her mind on the day before her instead of the night she had just spent. She had discovered on getting up this morning that she had sliced the bottom of her foot cleanly on the broken glass, a deep cut which did not bleed much. She studied it for any sign of infection before putting on her sandals, but it remained a thin, red line and she dismissed it.

They sniffed perfume, groaned over exquisite jewelry and Ivy was unable to resist trying on a wisp of peach- and rust-colored chiffon that would probably land in her wardrobe at home unworn.

"It's you. You simply must have it, Ivy," Zanne told her, holding out the stopper of a bottle of French perfume for Ivy to sample.

Ivy protested weakly, already resigned to having the dress. She bought a tiny bottle of scent, as well, and followed Zanne out to the car, only partly hearing the bright chattering voice going on about every woman's need of a dress that was purely impractical.

"You won't even know you have it on. For a tent that

hangs from a couple of spaghetti straps without ever touching base, it does marvelous things for your figure. Not that it needs any help."

As they dodged a woman and child on a motorcycle and headed out of town, Ivy was remembering the velvet caftan and what had happened the last time she wore it. Impractical was right! At this rate, she'd be broke before she left the island.

At lunchtime, Hunter announced his mission accomplished. Homer Varga stayed long enough to drink with them, but refused lunch, pleading a waiting wife, and Zanne was all apologetic, demanding to know why he hadn't brought his wife along to visit with her and Ivy.

"She's staying in Christiansted with some friends who were to leave this morning, Mrs. Orsini, but thanks all the same."

"Well, take her to the beach and let her soak up some sun before you go back to Chicago," Zanne insisted, fluttering around refilling glasses from the tall pitcher of rum-fruit drink.

"Yeah, don't forget the traditional tourist bit," Pete joined in. "Cameras, perfume, liquor, a suitcase full of damp, sandy clothes and a second-degree sunburn. It's traditional."

As they saw Homer Varga off in his rented car, Hunter draped a casual arm across Ivy's shoulder, causing her to catch her breath painfully.

"I think it's about time Ivy collected a few more of her sunspots, too, don't you? Shall we try the beach or stay here at home this afternoon?"

There was a chorus of voices and Ivy was glad for something to cover her embarrassment. Hunter acted as if last night had never happened, but she could not forget how close she had come to surrendering to him completely. It was just another close encounter, a near miss, to him, she supposed, but to her it was devastating, something she would never forget. Chalk up one more memory for the hard winter ahead, she advised herself silently, following the others into the jalousied room where a chilled bowl of West Indies conch salad awaited.

As it turned out, they stayed at home, lounging around the pool, one or the other of them dropping in occasionally for a leisurely, cooling swim. Hunter did not go in the water, without making an issue of the reason, but he, too, donned brief trunks and stretched out on a chaise longue. It was all too easy for Ivy to study his potent masculinity and she found it hard to keep her eyes away from his long, leanly muscled body in the bare trunks.

As if sensing her eyes on him, he turned toward her once and asked if she had had a good night's sleep.

Certain that all eyes were on her, Ivy felt herself flushing. "Yes," she said shortly, sliding into the pool to swim in her barely adequate style up and down for several minutes. Her escape had not precluded her seeing the meaningful looks Pete and his wife exchanged.

At dinner Pete mentioned a meeting of the historical society and Zanne declared that Hunter and Ivy should come into town with them, even if they didn't want to sit through the meeting. Ivy was not particularly enthusiastic, but she decided to go along with the others.

They watched the sunset over the Caribbean, hoping for a glimpse of the famous green flash, and Ivy, wearing her new chiffon, slipped off her sandals to prop her feet on the rail. Her foot was beginning to ache just a bit, what with all the walking she had done in town, but she couldn't bring herself to mention it. There had been enough speculative glances from their host and hostess without giving them something else to think about.

"Hey, I've got an idea," Pete said after Zanne rejoined them on the patio. She had gone inside to change into something she considered more suitable for a meeting of the society, although Ivy could not see much difference between the turquoise, lime, and purple muumuu she shed and the pink, orange, and red long shift she replaced it with.

"I'm not sure I'm up to any of your good ideas," Hunter ventured. "I had a bit of a headache last night and if it offers more than a quiet stroll in the open air, you can count me out."

"Lovey, why didn't you say so?" Zanne exclaimed. "Pete, why don't we drop Hunt and Ivy off at our special beach. The moon will be full tonight and it's due to rise in about an hour. They can take it easy while we settle the affairs of Queeg's Mill."

Before Ivy could voice the protest that arose in her throat, Pete was herding them out to the station wagon. "Great, man! You haven't been there since . . . has it been five years? The old place is still not developed, thanks to an adamant old woman who wouldn't sell if her life depended on it."

Even had she the chance, Ivy was not sure she would have begged off. Her foot hurt, surely, but was that any valid excuse to pass up an evening with Hunter on a moonlit tropical beach? She acknowledged her own weakness for giving in to her desires and climbed into the backseat with Zanne.

"We'll be back here in about two hours at most," Pete told them some fifteen minutes later, as he pulled up to a heap of distinctive rocks at the edge of a paved parking lot. There were no other cars in sight and Ivy was beginning to have second thoughts, but it was too late now. She got out and took Hunter's hand, leading him along the well-defined trail that led to the beach. She was still more than a little embarrassed at conversation during the trip, Pete's comment that it might have been a good idea if Ivy had changed into her jeans.

"Why, don't be an old fool!" Zanne had spoken up from beside her. "Ivy's dress is perfect for a moonlight walk on the beach. I remember a few times when you thought even a chiffon scarf was too much."

"Don't give it all away, woman." Pete had laughed and Ivy was grateful for the cover of darkness as she felt her cheeks burn.

Nothing had been said between Hunter and Ivy, however, and now, as they came to the hammered silver of the ocean under the mottled full moon, Ivy could not remain quiet.

"Oh, Hunter, it's the most beautiful thing I've ever seen," she breathed, feeling his responsive tightening of fingers on her bare arm. "I'm going to drink it all in and save it so that I can take it out again and examine it when we get back home. I know I won't be able to believe it."

He didn't speak, but at the companionable feeling of his solid warmth beside her, some of the shattering embarrassment she had felt from last night drained away. After a while, when three ungainly birds flapped by, she described them to him and asked what they were.

"Pelicans." He stopped to roll up his pants legs. They had both left their shoes on the rocks beside the parking lot. "They look wonderfully ugly close up, but seeing them like this, in the moonlight, they can be beautiful."

"Everything is beautiful tonight," she vowed, jumping back as a wave slithered to a stop inches short of her bare toes.

"Let's head down the beach toward town. You can see the lights in the distance around the bend here." His hands touched the flimsy material of her dress as it drifted about her in a soft cloud. "Is this the dress you bought today? What's it like?"

Ivy described it to him and he let his hands find her shoulders, fingering the thin straps, and drop down to her waist before sliding from her hips. "What color is it?"

"It's a sort of peach and rust color, although it looks different in the moonlight."

They moved with unspoken agreement along the

hard, wet shore toward a heap of rocks Ivy saw looming ahead. When she described them to Hunter, he remembered them, telling her of the times he had come here before.

"With Pete and Zanne?"

"One or the other or both . . . usually."

There was a light note in his voice and Ivy fought down the illogical stab of jealousy. Zanne was probably at least five years older than Hunter, but she was a fascinating woman, all the same.

"I introduced the pair of them and stood as best man at their wedding," Hunter continued, catching her hand as they neared the rocks. He told her they reminded him of a huge turtle and dropped down onto the nearest one, leaving Ivy to join him or not. Before she could seat herself, he had slipped down to the sand, leaning his back against the turtle's shell, and she followed suit, appreciating the stored warmth against her back, hard and sandy though it was.

"I should have suggested we bring a blanket," he murmured after a while.

"I'm glad you didn't," Ivy said quickly.

"Why? Did it embarrass you, what Zanne and Pete thought?"

"I'm not sure I know what they thought," she prevaricated.

"Of course you do." His voice was a combination of amusement and derision. "They brought us here to give us an opportunity to make love."

"Oh . . . don't be so ridiculous!" Ivy choked.

"Is it so ridiculous then? I thought it rather obvious."

"We could just as well have waited for them at home, in that case," Ivy snapped, then, catching her own double entendre, she stammered, "I didn't mean . . ."

Hunter laughed, his head thrown back against the bright night sky. "No, my sweet, I know you didn't. It would be beyond you to hint that a bed might be more civilized under the circumstances."

They were silent for a while and gradually Ivy

recovered some of her precarious poise. She suspected Hunter had allowed her time for just such a reason. When he spoke again it was to ask her to describe what she saw and what she thought of it, which she did, and then went on to discuss the differences in the skies here and back home in North Carolina.

"I never knew a sky—the same sky, really—could be so different," she exclaimed, settling down into the warm sand with absolutely no thought to the dress she had paid two weeks' salary for only hours before.

"How do they affect you?"

"How do you mean?"

"I mean what do you think about when you study something so abstract as a sky? You wouldn't think in the same terms as, say, a meteorologist, or a pilot . . . as I might, even. I was curious as to what went through your head under those circumstances."

She considered his question carefully before answering. "I think I grow philosophic," she ventured. "I mean, you can't just gaze at something so vast without thinking of your infinitesimal self clinging to the surface of a planet spinning in all that space. It could be frightening but somehow, it's not."

"Do you feel larger than life or smaller?"

"Oh . . . both, I guess. Physically one, spiritually the other, if you know what I mean."

"I suspect you've formulated a rather sound philosophy," he said thoughtfully. "One senses a . . . a sort of stability in you that's unusual for one so young. Unusual in anyone, for that matter, in my immediate social circle."

There was something in his voice that made Ivy study him in the bright darkness, searching for a clue to his thoughts. They were not touching, his own hands sifting idly through the sand while hers were clasped in her lap. She wondered what he would do if she laid her head on his shoulder and the very thought made her pull away slightly, as if on guard against some errant part of her own nature.

"I'd like to make love to you, Ivy," he said without turning toward her. He sounded as calm as if he were offering her a sweater against the night air.

She could think of nothing at all to say as she stared at him, stunned. Her heart had lodged somewhere in her throat and was only now resuming its fluttery beat again.

He turned to her then. "It's unbearable, not being able to see to judge your reactions. Maybe I should have acted instead of spoken."

When she could still think of nothing to say, even if she could have managed to get the words out, he reached for her, fumbling in a way unusual for him. His hand struck her clumsily on the breast and she flinched.

"Oh, Ivy . . . did I hurt you?" Surer hands now moved to her shoulders and followed up to her throat, her face, and he turned it to him as if to study it through the black silk band. His face looked somehow fleshless in the moonlight, its lean contours strange and unfamiliar.

"I'm all right, Hunter," she breathed shakily. Her muscles were tensed and there was a slightly dizzying pounding in her ears.

He drew her closer, practically breaking her in two as he disregarded physical limitations to turn her to him. Shifting awkwardly, Ivy was able to fit herself against his chest, her knees drawn up at his side, and when his mouth came down over hers, she abandoned herself to the utter physical delight of the moment. Her arms worked their way around him, one sliding over his shoulder to tangle in his hair and the other holding his hard, lean waist.

Without knowing quite how it came about, she found herself lying on the sand, his weight pressing her down until she could feel every hard contour of his body. His mouth left her own to search out the nerves along her throat, sending alarming messages to her most secret places, and she groaned when she felt his hands tugging at the flimsy fabric of her dress.

"I want to see you in the moonlight," he growled softly as he slipped the chiffon sheath over her unresisting arms and tossed it aside.

"How can you see me?" she cried, hardly recognizing her own husky, throbbing whisper. She knew irrevocably that just as she belonged to him mind and spirit, she would soon belong to him physically, as well.

"I can see you clearer than I've ever seen anything in my life."

After endless moments, his mouth left the chill, white mound of her breast and he stood, tearing off his shirt to toss it aside as he had done her dress, and when he unfastened his buckle and stepped out of his white jeans to stand before her in revealing briefs, she knew her decision was a foregone conclusion.

Her arms welcomed him as he reached for her again and the warmth of his long, hard body burned against her cool flesh.

"Ivy?" he whispered against the corner of her mouth, the question needing no verbalizing.

There was no tomorrow, no yesterday, only now, now and this driving, aching need to know the fullness of his love.

"Say it, darling," he urged. "I want so badly to hear the words. . . . I want you so. Please, tell me. . . ."

"I . . ." A voice inside her cried out that she loved him, but when the words were released on the still, soft tropical air, they shied away from the full truth.

"I want you, too, Hunter. Oh, darling . . . please . . ." She broke off, fighting an unreasonable urge to cry as she buried her face in his pulsating throat.

For a long moment, he held her there, neither of them speaking, both profoundly aware of the hammering of two hearts that together seemed to shake the very earth they lay on.

It was only as he lifted himself away from her, allowing the air to strike her face, that she realized her cheeks were wet.

Tenderly, almost reverently, he stood and helped her to her feet. Then, as if he were the sighted, she the blind, he led her with a strong arm about her naked waist, to the edge of the whispering surf. They stood there, bodies bare except for white, gleaming briefs, and let the warm water splash up on them.

Ivy gulped back her sobs, helpless to stem the flow of tears, and Hunter held her hand silently, standing slightly apart now.

"I'm afraid I can't offer you a handkerchief," he said ruefully as she began to get her breathing under control once more.

She laughed shakily and squeezed his hand, unable to get a word past the painful lump in her throat even if she had known what to say to him.

After a while she led him slowly back to where their clothes lay in the sand and handed him his shirt and trousers and they both shook the sand from them before putting them back on.

Oddly enough, there was not the slightest bit of embarrassment in her, nor, she was somehow certain, in Hunter. It was as if they had passed beyond that, to a deeper, quieter place, by the very denial of their passion.

By the time Pete and Zanne pulled up in the parking lot beside the rocks where they waited, Ivy was resigned to the fact that Hunter had remembered Evelyn in time to prevent his being unfaithful to her in the fullest sense. She was relieved, despite her aching disappointment, for had he taken what she so willingly offered, he would have been less than the honorable man she knew him to be. Ironically, his very denial of their mutual desire made her love him all the more.

Pete drove them to the airport the next morning and let them out, apologizing for not being able to stay and see them off.

"Dentist's appointment," he excused himself, stacking their bags inside the door. After assuring himself that Ivy could cope with the details, and inviting them both to come back anytime, he waved good-bye and left.

Ivy checked the luggage, leaving Hunter standing by the door, and as she turned back to join him, she was rocked back on her heels by the sight of Evelyn Carlin bearing down on him.

"Really, Hunter, do you do it on purpose?" Evelyn exclaimed shrilly, drawing herself up to a furious height as she came to a halt within inches of her fiancé. Hunter, to Ivy's alarm, looked almost ready to pass out. Without knowing she had moved, she found herself approaching them, ready to ease him into a chair should the need arise.

That the other woman had eyes for no one else was obvious, as was her anger, for her voice could be heard by everyone in the waiting room and there were quite a few interested faces turned their way.

"I've been here since day before yesterday and I've called every hotel on the island looking for you! There were seventeen Smiths registered in Christiansted and even an H. E. Smith in Davis Bay, which took almost a whole day to check out! I don't mind telling you, I could cheerfully strangle you at this moment! How could you do this to me?"

Hunter had regained some of the color that had fled his face at the first tirade so Ivy edged away to sit down behind a large woman laden with shopping bags bulging with plunder. She could not avoid hearing the furious words, however, and she learned that Evelyn had followed them as quickly as she could obtain reservations, intending to join Hunter so that Ivy could return home. She had hoped to persuade him to stay on for an extended vacation and it had taken all her money to search the island for him, as she hadn't counted on having to settle her own hotel bill.

She made no bones about allowing him to pay her way, Ivy thought disparagingly, before she remembered that she, herself, was as guilty of that as Evelyn.

Still, hers was an earned salary, even if she hadn't done much to earn it lately.

"The only thing I could do was to check up on when you were due to fly out of here and when I found out you had reservations for today, I changed my own so I could at least fly back with you."

Ivy's heart sank. Logic told her she had not a leg to stand on in her objections to the other woman's joining them, but disappointment sat like a cold rock on her heart.

She gathered up her purse, traveling case, and the extra shopping bag and prepared to board the plane when she heard their flight called. Her help would not be needed now, she saw, as she watched Evelyn lead Hunter aboard, making rather more of a production of it than was strictly necessary.

Chapter Seven

The flight home was a series of small humiliations for Ivy. The plane was crowded, but due to a bit of fancy maneuvering by Evelyn, Ivy ended up sitting in tourist class while Evelyn took her seat in the first-class compartment beside Hunter.

Not that Ivy wasn't glad of it before they finally reached Miami, for she disgraced herself by being airsick and not even the spectacle of following the sunset west made up for her utter misery.

If she could have arranged it, Evelyn would have accompanied them all the way, but she left the plane in Atlanta, promising to join them at Rougemont as quickly as possible.

It was unbelievably cold by the time they reached Smith-Reynolds Airport. As they bumped along 421 in the jeep, Ivy felt as if her nose, fingers, and toes would drop off. She sneezed, drawing a mumbled God-bless-you from Hunter. She wondered what was wrong with him. He had hardly spoken a word since Atlanta and she couldn't decide if he was missing Evelyn badly or if he was angry with herself, for some reason.

Of course, he could be embarrassed still at seeing Evelyn so soon after losing control on the beach, but if Ivy could come to terms with it, surely he could. Even if he had no idea that she loved him, he was experienced enough to accept the potent reality of physical attraction. He wouldn't be the first, nor the last man to succumb to the attractions of a soft, tropical night and a willing partner.

She ventured a comment after a while, in an attempt to ease the brittle atmosphere. "Do you think it's possible for the blood to thin out in only four days? I don't think I'll ever be warm again."

"What?" He made a visible effort to bring his attention around. "No. The world might flip on its axis in four days, but I don't think blood could thin out. It's this jalopy of yours. You should have taken the Jensen."

"This jalopy, as you call it, is yours, not mine, and while it may be slightly draftier than the Jensen, at least it won't run away with me. I'm not ready for all that horsepower."

He grinned and she felt herself thaw out a little. She had been sitting rigidly without realizing it for so long that she was beginning to ache all over.

It was late afternoon and a watery sun was hanging just over the tops of the trees; but for all the warmth it spread, it might as well have been midnight. The sky was dark with heavy-bellied clouds and a fine mist was beginning to fall, glistening ominously on the black branches of the trees along the sides of the highway.

The windshield wipers cut a monotonous swath as Ivy wished she had had something done about the heater. It had been out for almost a month now, but she had forgotten to mention it.

"I'm afraid we're in for an ice storm," she murmured, half to herself.

"What?"

"Ice storm," she repeated, raising her voice over the roar of the engine. "I said I'm afraid we might be in for one. It's beginning to stick on the trees and at Rougemont we're even higher than this."

They turned off 421 and took the narrow, rolling secondary road to the burned oak—the blasted oak, as Bill called it—where she turned again onto the unpaved state road and began to climb.

Hunter remained wrapped in his own thoughts, which was just as well, for Ivy needed all her concentration for her driving. The windshield was beginning to ice over and once she felt the jeep fishtail when she touched the brakes.

"Keep on moving," Hunter ordered her. "Don't worry about speed, we're not in all that big a hurry. Just maintain a nice, steady pace and you'll be all right. Luckily, there's never any traffic on this road."

He reached across and squeezed her thigh in what she supposed was meant to be reassurance. Even under such atrociously unromantic conditions, she thought with amazement, his touch still had the power to quicken her breath with a pain that seemed to grow worse all the time.

They were within a mile of home when something dark darted across the road ahead of them. Ivy slammed on the brakes, feeling the jeep veer sickeningly before it came to rest at an odd angle.

"Are you all right?" Hunter demanded roughly, fumbling with his seat belt. "What happened?"

"Oooooowsh!" Ivy let out her breath in an audible rush as she began to feel for the door latch. Something was definitely out of kilter; she'd better take a look before she tried to crank up the engine again. She opened her door, telling Hunter what she was about to do, then listened to a string of profanity that must have raised the temperature several degrees before she cut him off with a few sharp words of her own.

"Look, shut up, will you? Something ran across the

road right in front of my bumper and the rest was just reflex action. It doesn't help matters at all for you to yell at me, so kindly stow it while I get out and see what's wrong with this thing. I know we're not supposed to be tilted back at this angle."

Hunter was outside before she could even get a foot out the door and she saw his hands go to his blindfold.

"No!" she screamed. "Hunter, you wait right there and don't move!" She scrambled down and ran around the front of the jeep, hoping she had thrown a scare into him, because she had the terrible feeling he was about to rip his blindfold off. "Now," she breathed, reaching him within seconds, "if you'll just relax, I'll look the situation over and tell you what's going on. As far as I can see, there's nothing drastically wrong, we just skidded a wheel over into the culvert and I . . . Rinny!"

The low whine had alerted her and when she saw the dog cowering in the bushes across the drainage ditch, tail between his legs and that pathetic expression on his canine features, she groaned. "You old wretch! It was you that got us into this mess!"

"Who the hell is Rinny and would you please tell me what's going on? We're both getting drenched, in case you hadn't noticed."

"No, believe it or not, I hadn't, and Rinny's a dog."

"What's a dog doing running loose out here? There's not a house for miles except for Rougemont," Hunter exclaimed irritably. Then, in a different tone, "Rougemont. Ivy?" The suspicion in his voice grew threatening as he reached out for her but Ivy brushed aside his hand and grabbed his arm, urging him back inside the jeep. Then, with a helpless shrug, she managed to push the willing, but uncoordinated hound into the back seat. She climbed in under the wheel, shivering and blowing on her hands.

"What an odor! I take it you've put that beast in here with us, Ivy? I think you have a little explaining to do."

For some unfathomable reason, Hunter did not sound nearly as angry as he had only minutes before and Ivy peered at him through the miserable darkness. She told him, almost relieved to be able to confess, about the panhandling old mongrel who had turned up a few weeks earlier and made himself at home, wheedling her out of scraps with his sad, golden gaze and limp, ingratiating tail.

Sensing that he was the subject of conversation, the dog made a clumsy effort to join them in the front seat and Ivy pushed him away, not wanting a wet tongue adding to her discomfort. Rinny was lavish with his affections and his timing was not always the best.

"And you call him Rinny, short for RinTinTin, I suppose. Such originality."

"You're not angry with me?"

"That you took a flea-bitten mongrel into my house, made a pet of him and fed him my food? Sweet-talked the mutt and let him wreck my jeep miles from home on a night like this? Why, Ivy, why should you think I might be angry?" The sarcasm was overdone and Ivy succumbed to a giggle. Then, before she could say anything, she sneezed again and it was back to the business at hand; namely, getting the jeep out of the ditch and themselves back to Rougemont before conditions worsened.

In the end, they walked, with Hunter's arm draped across Ivy's shoulder and the dog trotting gracelessly along behind them. The sleet had begun to drive down with a punishing force now and Ivy kept her head averted as much as possible. Her eyes still watered but she did her best to direct them along the smoothest portion of the rough road. Twice Hunter stumbled and it was all she could do to remain on her feet, one of which was beginning to trouble her more than a little.

After several minutes of no sound except for the keening of the wind and the unrelenting rustle of the sleet, Hunter spoke suddenly. "You're limping. Ivy?

Did you hurt yourself back there?" he accused, gripping her shoulder with crippling force.

Beyond prevarication by now, Ivy told him the truth. "I cut it yesterday . . . day before yesterday, or whenever."

"On the beach?" he demanded.

"No, not on the beach," she flung back. "In your bedroom, if you must know! Now, can we go on? My foot probably won't kill me but this ice very well might if you're inclined to hang about all night in the middle of the road!"

Hunter's arm went around her waist and she could feel his support as they blundered along through the driving, icy rain. After an eternity, he paused; Ivy lifted dull eyes to him. "We're almost there," he told her.

"How can you tell?" It was pitch dark and Ivy could barely make out the surface beneath their feet.

"The sound has changed, can't you hear it? The house and the trees around it have blocked the wind. Come on."

Amazed at his uncanny perception, she listened and, indeed, there was a difference. She had simply been too numb to notice.

They had brought with them only the toilet articles they needed for the next day or so, because as Hunter had reminded her, they would not be needing their holiday clothes. Ivy unlocked the door with frozen fingers and let them into the house, slamming the door thankfully behind her.

"Golly, it's almost as cold in here as it is outside," she shivered. "I'll turn up the thermostat and you get out of those wet things. Rinny . . . into the kitchen, my friend. I'll see to you later."

She was crossing the hall as she spoke, peeling off her wet coat and wondering if she would be warmer with it or without. She turned up the thermostat at the same time she flipped the light switch but nothing happened. Sensing her next movement useless, she wiggled the switch nevertheless and ran the thermostat all the way up; it was no use.

"Hunter," she wailed, "the power's off. No lights, no heat. And no hot coffee and no bath," she added despairingly.

Under Hunter's direction, they got the fire going, put a kettle of water on the hearth, and changed into heavy bathrobes before the fire. At least, Ivy thought wryly, there was no need for false modesty when it came to changing clothes together. It would take more than a blindfolded man to make her budge away from the only warm spot within miles.

The first cup of coffee was barely lukewarm. From the looks of the rapidly blackening kettle, the next would be flavored with smoke, but she didn't care. At least it was warm, and at Hunter's insistence, she had laced both cups liberally with brandy.

"It's harder on you than it is on me, poor girl," Hunter pointed out as they huddled under blankets on the sofa before the blazing fireplace.

"How's that?" she asked hoarsely. Her throat was getting distinctly scratchy by now and both her head and her foot ached.

"I'm used to the dark. Maybe I'll lead you out to the kitchen after a while and let you guide me in gathering up something that can be cooked on a fireplace. The blind leading the lame, maybe, but we'd better face up to the fact that you're about to come down with a bad cold."

Between them they managed a creditable supper of soup and sandwiches, but by the time it was ready, Ivy's appetite had fled. She wanted only to warm the core of ice that had her muscles clenched until she ached all over. It infuriated her to see Hunter, now dressed in flannel slacks and a black turtlenecked pullover, moving about as lithely as if it weren't about thirty-five damp degrees in the house.

"I'd g-give my eyet-teeth for a kerosene blanket,"

she chattered, thinking longingly of the electric one on her bed upstairs.

"Or a gas stove."

"Or any kind of anything th-that would warm me up," she moaned despairingly, huddled deep in her blanket in the wing chair.

"There's only one answer to that. We sleep down here by the fire and I'll promise to keep you warm if you'll keep the fire stoked up. While I'm perfectly capable of the one, I'd hate to attempt the other, under the circumstances."

It was a measure of Ivy's misery that she didn't argue with him. She dimly recalled having made a few vainglorious resolutions about being the perfect nurse and housekeeper for the next few weeks, cool, efficient, and reserved, and here she was thinking longingly of crawling into bed with him. Even more ironic, her thoughts were entirely on her own creature comforts instead of more intimate matters.

She sneezed again and took his blessing for granted.

Perhaps she had been a little hasty in evaluating her responses, she thought later, as, wrapped snugly in Hunter's arms, she burrowed down in the heap of blankets on the floor in front of the fire. When she had hobbled upstairs earlier to drag out all the covers she could find as well as her heaviest flannel gown and two pairs of woolen socks, she had been thinking only of the delicious possibility of getting warm again.

Hunter had greeted her with the news that he was about to take care of her foot.

"You don't have to do that," she protested crossly, staggering under the load of warm woolens and quilts.

"Seeing as how I was more or less responsible for the damage," he pointed out provocatively, "it's the least I can do."

There was nothing she could say to that; she was only glad he couldn't see by the weak light of her flashlight the color that flooded her face. At his instructions, she dumped her load and rounded up the first-aid kit from the kitchen as well as a basin, into which she poured warm water from the kettle.

Peeling off her sock and slipper, she eased the foot into the pan while Hunter knelt before her. He laid a cool hand along the sole of her foot and announced a certain degree of inflammation.

"It's not burning up, but there's definitely something going on there. You were a fool to let it go this long. Why didn't you ask Zanne for disinfectant and a bandage?"

"Well, for one thing, I had told Pete I heard something in your room break during the night and he might have been a bit curious if I had showed him the evidence," she snapped, too uncomfortable to mince words.

Hunter grinned that slow, infuriating grin of his and Ivy, in spite of her anger, thought, "This is sheer lunacy!" How could she fight against her own feelings when they were living in each other's hair this way?

Now, with Hunter's even breathing against her back and his hand splayed out disturbingly across her stomach, she found herself unable to relax enough to get to sleep. It had pricked her ego, even feeling as miserable as she did, that for all he seemed to care, she might as well have been a hot-water bottle. Or Rinny.

Rinny! She had forgotten about the dog and there had been no sign of him when she had last been in the kitchen. She stirred, twisting her head around to peer at Hunter. Here in the darkness, he had taken off his blindfold and he assumed a curiously defenseless look without it. Rather like a man who has worn glasses all his life, when seen without them.

"Hunter," she whispered. The arm about her middle tightened and he flickered a small smile, but still he did not waken.

"Hunter, wake up," she prodded.

This time there was more of a response. The hand slipped up almost carelessly and cupped her breast and her heart suddenly leaped to her throat. "Hmmmm? What is it, love?" he murmured against her ear as his fingers moved slowly across the flannel-covered flesh. Her turgid nipple pressed aggressively against his palm and she could have died!

Trembling, she pulled herself away and glared down at him in the dim, flickering light. As he opened his eyes and looked steadily back up into her face, she gasped.

"Hunter, you shouldn't!"

"Are you protesting the use of my hands or the use of my eyes?" he teased, stretching his long, lean body beside her.

"Your eyes. That is, both!" she corrected, unable to get enough of the sight of his face without the baffling black band.

"I've been more or less easing out of total darkness for the past week or so," he informed her quietly. "No problem. I'll cover up again before daylight. Now, what woke you up?"

"I haven't been to sleep," she confessed before she could prevent herself. "But what about Rinny? Where is he?"

"The last time I saw him—figuratively speaking, of course—he was scratching at the back door, so I let him out. If he devoured that pan full of food you were collecting on the sink for him, he won't be hungry again for a week."

"But he'll freeze!"

"Where do you think he's been sleeping while we were gone?"

"I don't know. Irma's, I guess," she said sulkily.

"Then if he's cold, he'll go back to Irma's. Lie down and go to sleep, sweet. You don't have to take care of the world's strays single-handed, you know."

She settled herself warily down beside him, aware of

the tremulous fluttering of her own pulses. She only hoped he was not aware of how disturbing she found it, to be sleeping here beside him like this.

Hunter's breathing had long since resumed its slow, even tempo and Ivy was all but asleep when she heard his soft murmur against her hair. At the words, "Good night, my precious," she stiffened slightly, but was too far gone in sleep to do more than tuck the words away in her mind.

Morning brought a fairyland of ice-frosted trees, with each blade of grass sporting its own crystal coat in the blinding sunlight. Unfortunately, Ivy was in no condition to enjoy it.

When Hunter shook her awake to announce the resumption of electrical service, she could only croak a feeble question.

"If you're trying to ask me how I knew, poor old girl, I heard the furnace come on and assumed the rest. My blinder was in its proper place before the sun came up, in case you're concerned. And now, if you can manage to get out to the kitchen and be my eyes, I'll put together some breakfast for us."

What Ivy wanted more than anything else at the moment, other than to draw a painless breath, was a bath, but she made do with a hasty wash and tottered out to where she could hear Hunter bumping around in the kitchen.

"You'd better sit down before you break a leg or poison us or both," she advised hoarsely.

"I did manage to get some water on to heat. You must have hidden the bread, either that or we're out of it."

"It's in the freezer. The stuff doesn't keep forever, you know."

"Save your voice for essentials. Just put things in my hand and I'll do the rest. Yell if I'm about to commit a disaster. How's the foot, by the way?"

"Better, I think," she replied grudgingly.

There was something about his obvious blooming health as well as his insufferable high spirits that made Ivy feel even more disgruntled so she sulked until they managed to put together enough to stave off starvation. She had no appetite, anyway, but she was dying of thirst and her throat cried out for something warm and soothing.

After breakfast Hunter insisted she go back and lie down on the sofa. She protested she could go to her own room now that they didn't have to depend on the fireplace for heat, but he would have none of that.

"Look, whether or not you want to admit it, we're going to have to look after each other and the only way we can do that is if we stick together. Now, shut up and hand me the whiskey and, honey, see if we have a lemon. I'm going to fix you something for your throat and then I'm going to dress your foot again and that should do you until Bill gets here."

"Bill! Is he coming?"

"I called him first thing this morning while you were still tossing and muttering in your sleep. Remind me to tell you sometime what kind of a bedfellow you are."

Ivy felt dreadful. She hadn't had a bath since before they left St. Croix, she was dying of a sore throat and heaven knew what else, and he had to see her like this—well, if not see her, sleep with her, which was worse. One hand wandered aimlessly up to her head, perhaps in an effort to contain the ache that was rapidly making itself felt, and her fingers grated over sand on her scalp. In spite of all her shampooing the morning they had left, she had missed some of it.

"I've still got sand in my hair," she grumbled.

"Consider it a souvenir."

"I don't need any souvenirs, thank you."

"No, nor do I. I've an idea it will be a long time before I forget that particular trip," he said in a curiously bleak tone.

She looked at him, her head tilted to one side, but she could not fathom the feelings behind the enigmatic face he bent over the sink, as he splashed suds onto the floor.

He was making a valiant effort to spare her work and all she could do was grumble at him.

"Hunt, I feel like the devil. I'm going to get a bath and sleep until I either die or get well. Will you be able to manage for a while?"

"I promise you I won't venture off the beaten track. I may go over the tapes from the Varga meeting, but if I do, I'll close the door so I won't disturb you. Go on, get your bath, honey, and when you get back downstairs, I'll dress your foot for you. You'd better get yourself an aspirin or two, while you're at it. I can't trust myself to locate the right bottle for you."

Her very skin was sore. Her head was under control now, thanks to the pills, but her throat was raw and she felt distinctly weepy. It was all she could do to resist falling into her own cool, clean bed, but she reminded herself that Hunter was not above coming upstairs to find her if she didn't turn up in a reasonable length of time. His bullheaded arrogance was second nature and she was in no condition to meet it at the moment.

By nightfall her throat was better, her head merely dull, and the inflammation in her foot under control. She decided she was going to survive. Although she still had an occasional chill and felt as if the block of ice in her middle was still unthawed, at least she was hungry enough to heat a can of soup for them and to dig out cheese and crackers. Not a feast, but then Hunter, who was being as helpful as he could be under the circumstances, was also being extremely tolerant.

"Bill called while you were asleep," he told her over coffee after they had demolished the light meal. "Everything's still iced up and the roads are uncertain, but he'll try to make it by noon tomorrow. Meanwhile, he says for you to get plenty of rest, plenty of liquids, stay warm, and keep off that foot. . . . Oh, also don't bug me—doctor's orders."

"Very funny," she croaked. "I've got on so many clothes I feel like a sausage and I'm still shivering. I think I may get drunk."

"I think you may not. I'll instruct you in the making of a proper toddy—two, in fact; then you can get in bed and stay there. I kept you warm last night and I can do it again."

When she began to tell him exactly what she thought of insufferably bossy men he held up a hand in protest.

"Please . . . don't try to thank me. In case you're worried, I assure you I never try to seduce young ladies with red noses. I find they always get wheezy when the heavy breathing starts."

"Oooooh!" Blind or not, there was a definite gleam in his eyes; she could see it as well as she could see that wicked grin. For some reason Hunter Smith was in high spirits and for the life of her she couldn't figure out why! Either the business deal he had put across had been even better than he had expected or he and Evelyn had mended their differences between St. Croix and Atlanta. He was certainly not the same man who had prowled around here for weeks making her life miserable on all but the rarest occasions.

"Look, if there's one thing I can't stand when I'm feeling miserable, it's a clown. What's with you, anyway? Do you enjoy seeing me suffer?"

"Oh, I don't know. Just youthful high jinks, I guess. Maybe it's the influence of your friend, Rinny."

"Has he been around today?"

"He announced his presence bright and early, looking none the worse for his night on the town, so you needn't have been so concerned last night. Not that I'm sorry, mind you."

"Beast!" Ivy muttered under her breath. She didn't mean the dog and she had an idea Hunter knew it "Did you let him in?"

"I sent him away with a bone. At least, it felt like a bone and he didn't refuse it. You've made him quite at home in the kitchen I take it. He seemed to miss your clandestine meetings."

"They were not clandestine! I . . . I just didn't want you to know in case you made me get rid of him," Ivy asserted.

"Oh, well, as it happens, I suspected something was going on," Hunter replied silkily.

"You mean you knew about him all along?" she cried, dismayed at all her unnecessary trouble in keeping the dog's presence hidden.

"I heard you out there talking to someone—something, shall we say—and drew my own conclusions. Anyway, your darling Rinny trotted off with my best wishes this morning and if I hear him I'll let you know, all right?"

"Thanks, Hunt. He's one of Mattie's old strays and when I called Irma—Mattie's daughter who lives across the river, down toward town—she said he spent half his time at her house. She said his name when he was with them was Toro, of all things."

"I think P.T. Barnum might be more appropriate," Hunter observed dryly.

"Why do you say that?" Ivy was at the door, on her way for another warming hot tub.

"There's one born every day. Didn't he say that?"

By nine-thirty Ivy was half asleep. She had taken some cold tablets that had made her drowsy, so she had been lounging about listening to the radio, while Hunter had spent the afternoon working. She felt slightly guilty, knowing it was part of her job to see that he did not work too hard, but he seemed to be thriving on it. Whenever he left the library this afternoon, he seemed to be riding some secret crest of satisfaction. Maybe the vacation had been what he needed, even though it really was a business trip. Certainly the slight bit of tan he had acquired had made the furrows in his lean cheeks far less noticeable.

Fine thing! She had brought back a sore foot and a

cold but he had come home with a devastating tan and a new lease on life.

She was reluctant to spread the blankets on the floor again, for it would be a blatant admission that she was expecting to share it with him and she was suddenly shy of this new person he seemed to have become. Hunter Smith at his brooding, bad-tempered worst was hard enough to resist; heaven help her with this easygoing new charm of his! He'd knock her pitiful defenses for a loop!

She settled down on the sofa. It held one with comfort, although she remembered painfully that on one occasion it had been quite adequate for two. She was almost asleep when she sensed his presence looming over her.

"Well?" she growled, turning onto her back to blink up at him.

"Well, I just wanted to be sure where you were. It would have been considerate of you to tell me, you know. I tiptoed carefully around the center of the floor, afraid I'd step on your hand or trip and fall into the fireplace."

"How did you know I was here?"

"Simple deduction. Your conscience wouldn't allow you to ignore my instructions completely and go to bed upstairs in case I broke a leg going after you. Right?" He sounded grim and Ivy pulled the covers up closer about her face.

"Something like that," she conceded cautiously. "Now, have I your permission to go back to sleep?"

"Sarcasm doesn't become you, Ivy. Besides, you're still chattering." He reached down and laid a hand across her forehead. "It's a matter of metabolism. You won't be really warm without an outside agent to help you."

"And what outside agent do you suggest, Dr. Smith? The cord to my electric blanket would stretch out across the floor at about knee level and I'd hate to have your neck on my conscience."

"They say suffering ennobles. I'd hate to see you get much nobler. Your disposition wouldn't stand for it." With a minimum of effort, he swooped down, lifted her up, and, trailing blankets, held her tightly against him.

"Put me down, Hunter! I think you've gone crazy! You can't . . ."

"I can't see. Period. That's the beginning and the end to what I can't do, so shut up and behave yourself. I'm going to take you to my room where a comfortable, warm double bed awaits and you're . . ."

"If you think I'm going to bed with you . . . !"

"What's so different about tonight?" His calm was infuriating and Ivy resumed her struggles to get down, only to be clamped in a painfully tight grip against a rock-hard chest.

"I didn't go to bed with you last night," she temporized through clenched teeth.

"No, you didn't. You slept with me. Shall we argue semantics or will you come along like a sensible girl and let us get some sleep? It's cold in here even with the furnace going full blast and the two back bedrooms, yours and mine, will be pretty uncomfortable. You may think you have your cold on the run, but I don't intend to have it to turn into pneumonia, especially as the roads are too icy for help to reach us. You're going to get plenty of rest and stay warm; I'm going to see to both, so just shut up and stop squirming!"

"My, aren't we masterful?" she jeered, helpless against his superior strength.

"One more smart crack and I'll show you just how masterful we are," he growled threateningly.

Long after Hunter's breath leveled off to a slow regularity, Ivy lay awake, staring into the darkness through burning eyes. There was something so utterly impossible about the whole situation. Here she had just come from a tropical island where she had come within a hair's breadth of surrendering herself to this infuriating man, only to have his fiancée show up and waltz off with him at the last minute, and now she was sleeping with him for the second night in a row and all he could do was offer to keep her warm! If this was love, it was a farce! Furthermore, it hurt like the very devil!

All the same, she admitted sheepishly to herself, it was toasty warm under the blankets. She felt herself relaxing for the first time all day. In the halfway world between sleeping and waking, she mused on the impossible situation in which she found herself. There had been times recently when she had been sure Hunter was beginning to care for her in more than just a surface, physical way; but if he did, could he lie there beside her and go to sleep like that?

And if he did, then what? There was still Evelyn; he was engaged to her. Hunter was not the sort of man to take back a proposal, once it was offered. Besides, she mused sleepily, how could a man prefer a short, freckled country girl to a sophisticated beauty like Evelyn? Just because Ivy, herself, saw her in less than a flattering light didn't mean that a man would.

Chapter Eight

Bill arrived shortly after eleven the next morning and he was not alone. Evelyn had taken the opportunity to hitch a ride up from Atlanta. As Ivy watched the older woman hurry into the hallway, shivering delectably in her full-length mink coat, she was glad she had cleared away the blankets from the living room and made an effort to put on enough makeup to hide her pink nose and watery eyes.

Bill pronounced her on the way to recovery, saying he did not think an antibiotic was called for as she seemed to have weathered the worst of her cold and her foot was on the mend.

"Could have been nasty, though. You ought to know better than to take chances with a coral cut like that. Meanwhile, just stay warm, get plenty of rest and drink fruit juices. . . . You know the drill."

Neither Ivy nor Hunter straightened him out about the source of her injury and Evelyn made no pretense of showing an interest in her welfare. She spent most of her time that first afternoon with Hunter on the sofa, and Ivy, feeling definitely de trop, made herself stay upstairs until dinner time.

Evelyn helped out in the kitchen; Ivy had to give her credit for that. She accepted Ivy's offer to wash up, but Ivy was made to understand that, other than the actual preparations of the meals, the housework was all Ivy's concern.

Hunter remained in the library all the following morning, coming out only for lunch before disappearing again to go over the tapes of the Vargo meeting. Bill grumbled about his overworking, but did nothing more tangible. It was left to Evelyn to voice her protest. She resented being treated, as she said, like the hired help, left to fend for herself, and Hunter, with a sigh, agreed to go for a drive with her after dinner.

Evidently, Evelyn had no hesitation in driving Hunter's high-powered car, but since she had moved in more sophisticated spheres, her driving experience would naturally exceed Ivy's. Ivy and Bill were left to listen to television, the reception being so bad they could not really watch it. Bill told her he had planned to take Hunter in for a checkup the following day and that he was pleased at the way things were going. He asked about their trip, but Ivy was surprisingly reluctant to discuss it. It had been an intensely personal thing, something she would always remember right up to the scene in the airport, and she felt that she might lose something of it if she shared any part of it with someone else.

Evelyn tackled her the next morning as Ivy was washing up the dishes from breakfast. Since it had taken her almost an hour to clear away the remains of last night's dinner, she had decided it might be easier to do the cooking herself; at least she would not dirty every pot and pan in the kitchen.

"Have you found another job yet?" Evelyn asked, sitting at the table touching up her fingernails.

"Not yet. I haven't really looked so far," Ivy confessed.

"Isn't it about time? You certainly don't plan to hang around here and make things embarrassing for us, do you? Hunt was kind enough to give you the St. Croix trip as a sort of bonus, hoping you'd get the idea and move on without any long, drawn-out leave-takings, but I see you haven't taken the hint."

"I wasn't aware that a hint had been given," Ivy insisted stubbornly. She was determined not to let the other woman rile her, despite the fact that her temper was never at its best after a cold.

"Oh, well, of course it wasn't certain that I'd be able to take care of him this month, but now that that's all fixed up, you're really rather redundant. I mean, even you must admit that it's too much to expect Hunter to have to look after you with your ailments. Men just don't take to that sort of thing. Believe me, I know."

"You're staying on, then?" Ivy tried to hide her dismay. There would be no reason for her to stay on if Evelyn were here to look after things.

"Well, the children are settled with Henry's niece and I can concentrate all my efforts on Hunter now. We might use the time planning where we're going on our honeymoon. Hunt has a place in Montreal and another at Cap d'Antibes. Of course, as a model, I'd really prefer Paris, but it will be awfully early in the spring."

Ivy wiped her hands on the apron and shoved her hair away from her face. Steam had caused the shorter tendrils to curl untidily.

"You'll be married as soon as his treatment is over?"

She didn't want to know the answer, but had felt this remark to be the only appropriate one. Since she couldn't just walk away without exposing her feelings she didn't wait for a reply but said neutrally, "If you'll excuse me, I think I'll go lie down. Bill said I should get as much rest as possible if I want to avoid trouble."

She did not specify what trouble she sought to avoid,

but she had an idea Evelyn was not fooled by her escape.

On impulse, she dialed Finley's number from the upstairs extension. There was really no point in putting off the inevitable and it had been inevitable right from the very beginning. If Ivy had fooled herself into thinking there might be a chance for her with Hunter, she knew better now.

"Hello, Finley? It's me, Ivy."

He was surprised to hear from her and Ivy thought she detected a trace of discomfort, but when she explained what she wanted, he was all cooperation.

"Look, girl, I might be able to help you about a job, but I won't know until sometime later on today. An agent I know in Winston-Salem might be able to use you. About a place to stay, you're in luck. At least, partly. I tried to call you all last weekend to tell you that Micki and I are getting hitched in Orlando, but there was no answer and I didn't feel particularly free to barge in on you again. Anyway, we're planning to take off tomorrow. Since the lease on my place doesn't run out until the last of the month, you're free to move in here if you'll take it as you find it. I won't feel compelled to clean up that way. Then, if you get the job in Winston, you'll have time to look around for an apartment."

By the time Bill and Hunter left for the hospital, Finley had still not called back. Ivy was determined to be gone before they returned. She had no desire at all to try to explain to Hunter why she was leaving with no notice before her time was up and, besides, she couldn't trust herself to remain unemotional should he question her. The aftermath of the past few days had left her feeling weepy and slightly irrational at the best of times.

As luck would have it, Finley called just as Evelyn came to ask her to run a load of washing and there was no way she could disguise her plans from the openly curious woman.

"That's great, Fin," she told him after hearing that she had an appointment on Monday morning to apply for the job of secretary to a realtor in Winston-Salem. "The only thing is, I don't know how I can get away from here. The jeep stays, remember? Besides, we just got it back from the garage and I don't have the nerve to borrow it."

On the other end of the line, Finley was explaining why he was not free to pick her up. He assured her that the apartment was hers until the end of the month if she needed it, although if she got the job in Winston, as he felt sure she would, she'd need to locate someplace there.

"If you can make it today, Ivy, just come on and I'll bunk in with Sam tonight. He's going with us to Orlando in the morning, anyway. . . . Got to be sure his little darling isn't left waiting at the altar. As if there was a chance of that."

"Congratulations, Fin. I always thought you'd make a beautiful groom," Ivy teased.

"All right, you handsome wench, see how many more favors I do for you! See you later, babe!"

As soon as Ivy put down the receiver, Evelyn launched into a series of questions. There was no reason to hold back and so Ivy admitted that she had a job prospect and a place to stay. All she needed now was a means of reaching them.

"But that's no problem," Evelyn exclaimed brightly. "I have the keys to the Jensen and Hunter trusts me with it, so why don't I take you wherever you need to go? How long will it take you to get ready?"

Whew! Ivy leaned back in her chair. Talk about the bum's rush! What had happened to the laundry that simply *must* be done? It was easy to see where Evelyn's priorities lay. Still, there was no reason not to take her up on it. It would certainly simplify matters.

"Would an hour be soon enough?" she asked tentatively as she ranged ahead in her mind, thinking of what had to be done.

"Make it half an hour and you've got a lift. I thought I might try to get my hair done this afternoon. Nobody in North Carolina knows how to do a decent job, of course, but beggars can't be choosers."

With a derisive glance at the sleek black cap of hair that fell to the gold-beaded choker Evelyn wore, Ivy shrugged. She hadn't sampled the beautician's talents, herself, but she knew plenty of girls who had, with results that equaled, if not surpassed Evelyn's rather extreme bob.

Thirty-five minutes later she stood in the hall with both her suitcases plus an assortment of odd packages, waiting for Evelyn to join her. Her conscience was beginning to plague her by now and she hesitated over whether or not to leave a note.

Evelyn made up her mind for her by calling downstairs to say that she'd be down in five minutes.

So much for her deadline, Ivy thought wryly. She walked decisively into the library and then was sorry she had. The sight of Hunter's untidy papers, his tape machine, and the chair he used all swept in on her with devastating effect. It occurred to her that the picture of her granddaddy, who had used that desk and chair all her life, had been replaced in two short months by another, more powerful vision. She could see him now, tilted back with all the arrogance of a Hanoverian prince, leveling her with one shaft from those piercing gray eyes, eyes that saw all too much even through a layer of black silk.

No, there was no doubt about it; she was wise to leave now, before she revealed too much of herself. While Hunter, himself, might be kind and compassionate about it, Evelyn would be scathing if she knew how far Ivy had fallen. She had seen those triumphant looks on several occasions and was not eager to sample any more.

Pen poised over a page from her stenographer's note

pad, she hesitated. What could she really say except that she was going, and that would be self-evident. That she was sorry? Why should she be sorry that Hunter's fiancée's coming to stay had made her presence unnecessary?

Suddenly, she began to write: Dear Bill, I've found a job and I'll be staying at the address below for a few days. Please do two things for me. . . . Call and let me know how Hunter's checkup was. This is the last, isn't it? And would you pack up my silver-working things in the shed and put them up in the attic? I'll manage to retrieve them as soon as I know where I'll be staying permanently. I've loved knowing you. Maybe someday we can get together again. Ivy.

She jotted down Finley's address and phone number just as she heard Evelyn clattering down the stairs, and looked around hurriedly for an envelope.

"Ready? What on earth are you doing?" Evelyn had appeared in the doorway just as Ivy pulled open a drawer that used to hold stationery.

"Looking for an envelope," Ivy said, defensive for no good reason.

"I don't think you have any business in here at all, much less going through Hunter's desk," Evelyn snapped. She was dressed in a couture suit of black and white with touches of cerise and Ivy felt small and grubby, kneeling down over the open drawer in her jeans and pullover. Under the circumstances, she had not thought it necessary to take time to change.

With a brief flash of angry resignation, she folded the note, wrote Bill's name across the front, and left it on the desk. Hunter would not be in any condition to read it and sooner or later it would come to Bill's attention. If it didn't, then it would not make that much difference.

Finley was out when Ivy arrived at his apartment. The place looked dismal. She had been there several times in the past but she had never been so aware of the worn vinyl tile and the grubby paint. Pale green had never appealed to her but when it was several years old, bearing the marks of nails and tape in the spots where Finley had changed his mind about the placement of his reproductions, it looked even worse. You'd think a realtor would have had more pride, Ivy thought without rancor as she looked with distaste at the rumpled bed.

By dark, she had done her best by the place and it looked considerably better. The beige-shaded lamps cast a flattering light around as she sat cross-legged on the floor, polishing a pair of shoes for her appointment. That was four days away, but she had to keep busy with something or her thoughts would not bear living with.

Finley came by at nine to throw a few clothes into a bag and take his leave of the place.

"You've really spruced it up, Ive. Good thing for me you came along. Look, I've got a footlocker packed and as soon as I get this bit done I'll be out of your hair. Micki's coming by later on, if it won't disturb you, to pack away a few dishes and things. We thought we'd leave the rest of the junk for the next tenant. If you . . ."

He broke off at the shrill summons of the phone and picked up the receiver. "Hello, Finley here."

There was a barrage of sound from the other end. Ivy saw a chagrined look cross Finley's face as he handed her the phone.

"Hello?" she ventured, half suspecting what was to follow.

It was Hunter and he was furious. Ivy listened helplessly as he described someone who would run out without even having the grace to say good-bye, much less giving a reasonable amount of notice. She tried to interrupt, to tell him why she had left . . . or to tell him as much as she wanted him to know, but it was no use. After several minutes of scathing attack, Hunter announced that he had something for her, that he'd see she got it, and then he slammed down the receiver.

"Whew!" She shook her head and leaned back,

averting her face slightly because she was in no mood to explain the wetness of her eyes.

"Caught it rough, huh? What's the matter, did he try Lancing's tricks on you? You know, Ivy old gal, maybe I overlooked something in you all these years."

After Finley left, Ivy cleaned up the shoe-polishing material and took a hot soak in a tub filled with fragrant suds. She needed all the help she could get tonight, she told herself, pouring herself a glass of too-sweet sherry. She balanced one of the three remaining wineglasses Finley had on the edge of the tub and switched on some music in the living room. The cheap transistor made the strains sound thin and harsh, but it was better than having to listen to her own thoughts.

Forty-five minutes later she was suitably drowsy, thanks to the alcohol and the warm water. She had remade the bed with fresh linen and now, in her short nylon gown, she thought she just might get through the night without too many dreams.

Then she remembered Micki; Finley had said she was coming by to pack some dishes. It was after ten now and if she didn't come soon, it would be too late. Ivy was not about to wait up for her.

She heard the pounding on the door as she was rinsing out her wineglass, since that might be one of the things Micki wanted to pack.

"Come in," she called out. "Be there in a second."

She dashed to open the door in case Micki hadn't a key but when she saw the grim, unrelenting figure standing there she was suddenly cast back some two months.

"Yes, it does seem like a repeat, doesn't it?" Hunter said harshly as Ivy fought against a weakness that threatened to overcome her.

"What do you want?" she whispered through stiff lips.

"Have I come at an inconvenient time?" His eyes dropped insolently down her body and she felt naked, in spite of the covering of white nylon. "Should I pay my respects to my host first?"

He pushed his way in, causing her to step back to avoid coming into contact with that rigidly held body, and looked around derisively.

"Anytime would be inconvenient, and there's no host here. Tell me what you want and then go, please, Hunter. I don't think we have anything to say to each other. You said your share on the phone," she told him bitterly. She braced herself against the powerful influence of his tall, forbidding presence. If she could just keep in her mind the hateful arrogant things he had told her on the phone, she might yet escape with her pride still flying.

"Aren't you going to offer me a drink? You don't seem as free with Hooper's hospitality as you were with mine," he remarked nastily. There was no blindfold now to shield her from the contempt in his eyes.

"I don't think you really want a drink and I . . . I . . . please, just say what you feel you must and leave!"

He moved closer without seeming to take a step. It was as if by sheer weight of personality he was crowding her against a wall.

Her knees came up against the edge of Finley's slightly sprung sofa bed and she flung up her arms to keep her balance.

Hunter grinned, a wicked, gleaming exposure of strong white teeth set off by cold, glowing eyes. "Were you expecting your lover? Did he have to go back to the office, maybe? You certainly swung open the door willingly enough, considering your lack of clothes."

"I thought it was Micki," she defended at once, trying to sidle away and having no success as he pressed her backward with his sheer bulk.

"Oh, Mickey, is it? My pardon, I thought you were moving in with Finley. Or do you take your lovers two at a time?"

"Micki is not . . . !" she began, to be cut off short by

the hands that gripped her shoulders. The pain made her wince, for there was none of the gentleness she had known before from him now.

"At least Evelyn had the good taste to take her men one at a time. Perhaps I shouldn't have been so hasty, but then, how was I to know that the sweet young woman who was so willing to give me anything I wanted on a certain beach a few nights ago was such an expert? Like the fool I was, I thought my experience in such matters had led you along a new road and I declined— not without a good deal of pain, I may say—to take advantage of your innocence. That's a laugh, isn't it? I should have trusted my first indication about you, Ivy de Coursey. Then maybe we would have made time fly during those first two months."

"Hunter, you don't know what you're saying," Ivy pleaded, her eyes round pools of green darkness. "Please . . . please don't say these things to me."

"You're right, my sweet. Why bother talking?" He brought her steadily closer to him, as if she were a mesmerized bird, until she could feel the hard heat of his body pressing into hers through the tissue of her gown. She twisted her head away from his relentless mouth, her very heart screaming a protest against his contempt, but it was no use. One of his hands came up under the weight of her auburn hair and caught her head, forcing her to meet his kiss.

Her lips remained clamped tightly together as she stood rigid in his embrace until he lifted his mouth slightly and whispered against her bruised lips, "So, you're going to fight me, but I know how to demolish those barriers, don't I? Shall I demonstrate?"

His tongue flicked out to caress her mouth as one of his hands moved along the silky flesh of her stomach and trailed fire until it captured her breast. With a contemptuous deliberation, he traced the swollen nipple through its film of nylon until her breath caught in her throat and her knees buckled against him. At her gasp, he plunged into a kiss that sought to wreck her very soul, and all too soon she was clinging to him, whimpering his name as he lifted his head to stare down at her.

Somehow his coat had dropped from his shoulders and now he tore a hand away from her palpitating body to rip the tie from his neck. Her trembling fingers did the rest. Opening his shirt to reveal the dark, crisply haired flesh beneath, she buried her face in his warmth, utterly undone by the powerfully aroused body that bore her down to the sofa bed.

"Ivy, Ivy . . . you tear me apart, sweetheart," he groaned in her ear as he moved to cover her body with his own.

She had no thought except for what was happening to her. . . . No thought for the future, none for the hateful words that he had flung at her moments ago. Her hands slid around him. Pulling the shirt from his belt, she dug her fingers into the hard, male strength of his back, wanting to draw him closer, closer to her, to ease this dreadful hurting ecstasy inside her. She had never known what it was to feel like this before she had met Hunter and even now, in her state of near delirium, she knew no man would ever be able to reach the inner core of fire that lit her soul and body as Hunter was doing now.

"Please . . . don't go. . . ." she pleaded mindlessly as she felt him lift away from her.

"I'm afraid my timing was off, darling," he whispered. Ivy stared up at him. There was something dreadfully wrong with the way his voice fell on her ears. In her ultrasensitive condition, she was aware of a thread of harsh contempt, a note of . . . pain?

"Hunter? What is it?" Her fingers slipped from his shoulders as he rose to stand before her, shirt opened on his magnificent torso. With a cruel deliberation, he picked up his coat from the floor and extracted an envelope from the inside pocket before slipping his arms into the sleeves. He tossed the envelope at her, flung his tie around his bare throat, and nodded coolly.

"One or the other of your lovers is on his way upstairs, my dear, and as this is the only door up here, I assume we're about to be visited. Too bad. You were beginning to show some promise."

As the door slammed behind him, Ivy thought she lost consciousness just for a minute. Surely, no pain could equal what ripped through her insides at that moment. She lay stunned for perhaps a minute, maybe more, and it was as if her whole life passed in front of her eyes. Only this was not her past; it was her future, a future without Hunter, and it was not to be borne!

"Ivy? It's me, Micki! Let me in!"

Somehow she managed to get through the ensuing hour. Her face hurt from the rigid control she exercised over it as she left Micki to her chore in the minuscule kitchen.

She was still awake when she heard the door quietly open and close. Only then did she give in to the tears that seemed to flow up from the roots of her very being. She had not missed the bright look of interest on Micki's face when she let her in; she knew the other girl was dying to ask about Hunter, but Ivy forestalled her. She could not bring herself to think about him, much less to speak his name.

Now she poured it all out; all the hurt, the agony he had brought with him, as if she had not left Rougemont with enough to last her half a lifetime.

By morning she was drained. But, amazingly enough, she was able to see the soon-to-be-married couple off with every semblance of cheer. It was only when she climbed the stairs and let herself back into the apartment that she saw the envelope on the floor beside the sofabed.

Curiously, with no sense of foreboding, she picked it up and slit the edge. Out fluttered a thin blue rectangle—a check.

"Oh, no!" she breathed, feeling behind her for a chair as the room began to spin around her.

It was a check for five thousand dollars, made out to

Ivy de Coursey and signed with Hunter's familiar aggressive hand.

She stared at it where it had landed on the vinyl floor for several minutes before picking it up and tearing it to tiny shreds.

On a day some two weeks later Ivy noted the date on the calendar that hung just inside the storeroom in the quick-food restaurant where she worked as a waitress. This was the day when Hunter's treatment was to have ended. She did not doubt that he had not worn the blindfold again after appearing at Finley's apartment without it almost two weeks ago.

She located the giant jar of mayonnaise she had come for and returned to the hectic kitchen. In half an hour she could begin getting ready to go home. Her feet looked forward to it, if her mind did not. As long as she could work constantly, a bright smile pasted on her face and the ready phrases on her lips, she didn't have time to think. It was later on, when she was at home in the one small room her paycheck would afford her, with her feet propped up on the head of the ugly veneer bed, that she had time to dwell on the past.

After completing her share of the nightly closing-up routine, she called a tired good night to the other workers. They were a young group, lively and good company. She was glad, in a way, that the other job had been taken by the time she applied. That way she had cut all ties with the past. There was nothing now to connect her to Rougemont, not even Finley's apartment which she had left the second day.

It was only a five-block walk to the house where she had obtained a room but Ivy did not particularly relish walking it alone at this hour of the night. So far, she had had no trouble, but she felt particularly alone and vulnerable at times like this.

Rounding the corner of the block where she lived, she pulled her collar up tighter around her neck. The wind whipped down that street as if it were a wind tunnel, for it faced the northwest and ran up a steep hill. It was a good thing she was basically a healthy person, or the dragged-out feeling that had followed her cold two weeks earlier could have flattened her with ease.

Her step quickened as she saw the square white asbestos-shingled house with the bare bulb lighting its front porch. Her landlady made that concession to Ivy's late hours, although she didn't hide her disapproval of them.

A dark shadow broke away from a car parked at the curb and moved toward her and Ivy's heart leaped into her throat. She eyed the front porch, tring to calculate how long it would take her to find her key and unlock the door. With all her muscles tensed, she heard her name called.

"Ivy?"

Stunned, she stared at the man who moved swiftly to prevent her escape.

"Ivy! Stop it!" Hunter's hands caught her shoulders and shook her as she tried to twist away from him. "Stop it, do you hear me? Come on!"

Before she could recover her speech, he had opened the door to the Jensen and shoved her inside, joining her before she could collect herself enough to get away.

"Now, let me tell you I had one hell of a time locating you. Don't you *ever* run away from me again." His voice had a quality of Toledo steel—except for a roughness that seemed to creep into the last few words.

"What do you want from me? Didn't you say enough the last time? Did you forget a few choice insults you might have used?"

"Oh, Ivy . . . it isn't enough to say I'm sorry, I know that. You'd never believe me and I wouldn't blame you. What I did . . . what I said was unforgivable, but if you'll just let me explain, I'll allow you to go wherever you want to go and never bother you again. I don't expect more than that."

She was silent, her eyes hanging on to his as if she were drowning and he were her only hope of salvation. When she did not speak, he sighed heavily and ran a hand across the back of his neck in the terribly familiar gesture. It was all she could do not to reach out to him.

"I never saw anyone disappear so quickly and so completely. When I saw the newspaper article and realized what a fool I had been, I went back immediately, but it was too late. You were gone and the landlord hadn't the slightest idea who you were, much less where you had gone."

In the pause that followed, she asked in a small voice, "What newspaper article?"

"The write-up of the marriage between Micki Mac-Neely and Finley Hooper," he told her bitterly. "Can you imagine what my thoughts were like at that moment? Knowing I had accused you of heaven knows what with both of them." He laughed shortly and the sound ripped through Ivy like a sword. He sounded as if he hated himself!

"Hunter . . ." she began, reaching a tentative hand out to touch his arm.

"No, don't take pity on me, Ivy. I'm no longer able to function with this boxcar load of guilt and until you hear me out, I can't even start to put myself back in working order. Ha! Here I am, taking from you again. Same old pattern, isn't it? I take whatever you offer and sometimes more than you're willing to give and give not a thing in return! How did you ever put up with me?"

"I didn't put up with you, as you call it," she said in a stricken voice. "Hunter, stop it! You don't have to say all this to me. You don't owe me anything—any apologies. I'm the one who left you without warning, remember?"

"And that's another thing. That check . . . which you haven't cashed, by the way. I was so sure you'd use it for your Florida honeymoon. The idea gave me a hateful sort of satisfaction."

"My honeymoon! What on earth are you talking about?"

"Oh, didn't I tell you? Yes, I thought you were living with Hooper until the pair of you moved south to get married—the idea promoted by my ex-fiancée, I might add. Then, when I discovered that not only were you not marrying Hooper, but the other man I accused you of having was none other than the bride-to-be . . . well, Ivy, can you imagine what I must have been through? And you were nowhere to be found! I couldn't even wipe that one off the slate!"

"But, Hunter, there was never anything like that between Finley and me," Ivy protested.

"I know that now. I got hold of Hooper in Orlando, thanks to the father of the bride, and he suggested I try the place he had lined up a job for you. I drew a blank there. They said the position had already been filled when you showed up, so I looked up a newspaper from that date and checked out every job advertised. It's taken me until tonight to get through all the secretarial and housekeeping positions. Luckily, the first restaurant I called was the one you had taken—the one that had taken you—and here I am. They gave me your home address."

"No one told me. . . . Mr. Cale should have told me."

"I asked him not to. Once I convinced him I wasn't a crank, he went along with the small surprise I said I'd planned."

"It was a surprise, all right." She laughed shakily. "I was ready to scream for help."

"I didn't know what else to do. I couldn't have waited another day to see you, Ivy. Ivy . . . I remember a time when you wanted to give me an explanation and I wouldn't hear it. You've been very generous. I don't deserve it."

When he turned away from her to face the front, his hands clenched tightly on the steering wheel, Ivy waited. It seemed as if that were all, though, and her heart grew heavy in her breast. She had begun to have a small flicker of hope, but she might have known that it was simply a matter of getting her off his conscience. No strings attached, wasn't that what he planned?

"Your treatment is over now, I suppose. I guess you'll be going back to Atlanta." She was proud that her voice betrayed none of the pain she felt at seeing him again just to lose him once more.

"The treatment ended when I came back from the hospital to find you gone," he told her bitterly. "Evelyn was full of plans for closing up Rougemont and spending the rest of the time at Highlands. She was sympathetic with me for losing my housekeeper, but, as she explained, how could we expect more when you and Hooper were getting married within a few days. She admitted playing Cupid and taking you to his apartment when he called and begged you to move in with him."

He struck the steering wheel with a clenched fist and turned to her again. "Blind! I didn't know what blind was when I asked Evelyn to marry me. She was . . . still is, I suppose, although I can't see it now . . . a beautiful woman. She led me to believe all she wanted was a father for her children and a chance to make a home for them and a husband. Well, I was ripe for the plucking." Again that harsh, bitter laugh. "Thirty-five, no family, no home except for a string of cold, impersonal properties and a regular line of hotel suites. The idea appealed to me and I asked her to marry me. From the moment the words were out of my mouth I began to have second thoughts, but what can a man do? I certainly couldn't say, sorry, I've changed my mind. Breach of promise didn't occur to me then, but it soon became a very real threat. I hoped she'd soon tire of the game, but I should have known better. When she told me that day last month that she'd finally decided to take me up on my proposal and shifted the ring to her left hand, I could have killed her. By then, you see, I'd already fallen hard for a little freckled country girl with more spunk and more integrity in her generous soul than I'd ever encountered before. Not to mention a body that drove me wild. Girl, you have no idea how many pitched battles I fought with myself over you! A little lighthearted lust would have been one thing, but I loved you, girl. . . ." His voice dropped to a husky growl. "I love you."

As if pleading for her understanding, he turned to her and in the strange glow of the mercury-vapor light, Ivy read the agony in his eyes that told her he meant every word he had said. The agony that had been echoed in her own heart up until that very minute.

"Hunter . . . Hunter?" she said tentatively, not knowing how to say what she wanted him to know.

"Anyway," he went on, a little unsteadily, "I laid my cards on the table and told Evelyn that I was planning to stay on at Rougemont, that I was through traveling except for an occasional pleasure trip, and that I did not love her. We went a few rounds, but in the end, she accepted a ruby-and-diamond necklace to match her ring and bowed out of my life. I don't think she was particularly interested in being a country girl."

"Then you'll be needing a housekeeper again, won't you?" Ivy ventured, her lips trembling with several emotions, amusement being only one of them.

"Are you applying for the position?"

"What are the fringe benefits?"

"It's a live-in job—a sleep-in job, for that matter. The hours are long, there's a lot of night work involved, and the boss is demanding. Not only that, but it entails a lifetime contract."

"What do you think my chances are of getting it?"

He held his arms open wide. "Here's where you apply," he told her, gathering her to him as if he could never get enough of the feel of her, the scent of her, the taste of her.

Several kisses later, he put her slightly away from him. The windows of the plush, understated car were completely steamed up. It was as if they were enclosed in a small, private cocoon, but it was not enough. "Come on, precious, we're going to get you packed and go back home."

"You can't go in there with me," Ivy protested, putting her clothing back in order and brushing away the hair that had fallen down. "My landlady is awfully straitlaced. If she thought I had a gentleman caller, I'd lose my room."

"The sooner the better." Hunter laughed, catching her to him for yet another kiss. "I have a much better room in mind and we can be there in about an hour if you get a move on."

The late-winter wind cut a frigid swath down the dark street as they got out of the steamy interior of the car, but neither of them noticed it at all.

Silhouette Romance

Buy one, get one free!

Save the cash receipt when you buy your next Silhouette Romance and mail it to us along with this coupon. By return mail, you'll receive another new Silhouette Romance *absolutely free!*

This offer expires July 31, 1981

Silhouette Romances, Dept. B-1F
1230 Avenue of the Americas
New York, N.Y. 10020

Please mail me my new, free Silhouette Romance.
I have enclosed the proof-of-purchase cash register
receipt asked for in this offer.

_____
NAME

_____
ADDRESS

_____
CITY   STATE   ZIP

CARMEN (handwritten)

READERS' COMMENTS ON SILHOUETTE ROMANCES:

"Every one was written with the utmost care. The story of each captures one's interest early in the plot and holds it all through until the end."

—P.B.,* Summersville, West Virginia

"Silhouette Books are so refreshing that they take you into different worlds. . . . They bring love, happiness and romance into my life. I hope Silhouette goes on forever."

—B.K., Mauldin, South Carolina

"What I really enjoy about your books is they happen in different parts of the U.S.A. and various parts of the world. . . ."—P.M., Tulia, Texas

"I was happy to see another romance-type book available on the market—Silhouette—and look forward to reading them all."

—E.N., Washington, D.C.

"The Silhouette Romances are done exceptionally well. They are so descriptive . . ."

—F.A., Golden, Colorado

* names available on request